THE FABRIC OF MURDER

The Ashmole Foxe Georgian Mysteries

WILLIAM SAVAGE

Published 2015

This is a work of fiction. All characters and events, other than those clearly in the public domain, are products of the author's imagination. Any resemblance to actual persons, either living or dead, is unintended and entirely co-incidental.

ISBN 978 1520215167

Ridge&Bourne
PUBLICATIONS

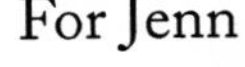

For Jenn

THE FABRIC OF MURDER

Chapter One

Mr. Foxe

IT WAS MR. ASHMOLE FOXE's invariable habit to take his breakfast at nine in the morning. He liked a substantial meal with fresh rolls, toast, cake, preserves and hot chocolate. Then, each day except Sunday, he left his house, promptly at ten, to walk to The Swan Coffee House below the marketplace. There he would occupy his usual place at a table in the corner and pick up the latest edition of the morning newspaper. Thus he would acquaint himself with whatever was happening in Norwich and the world beyond. Finally, he would turn the pages to find the advertisements placed by the many other booksellers in the city. He was always interested to see what each might be offering.

Norwich had many coffee houses. The Swan occupied a building from the time of Queen Elizabeth. Though it was spacious and the coffee was good, it was never noisy, as some were, filled with disputes and arguments. People here sat at their regular tables, met the friends they met yesterday and talked of habitual subjects in quiet voices. A raised arm was sufficient to call a waiter. The chairs were comfortable and the room warm, even in winter. It was not unusual to see that one or two of the older denizens had fallen asleep over their newspapers.

There was no doubt that Mr. Foxe was a bookseller. What manner of bookseller was harder to define. His shop, on the ground floor of the building where he lived, was open for business only on one or two afternoons. A casual visitor would find the shelves within stocked mostly with books of an ordinary sort. Taken all together, they might be worth fifteen or twenty pounds. Probably less.

Yet Mr. Foxe dressed like a gentleman. He kept five servants – a housekeeper, who also did his cooking, a housemaid, Molly, his manservant, Alfred Horsfall, plus a scullery maid and a chambermaid for cleaning. He occupied the whole of the building above and behind the shop. It was even rumoured that he owned the premises.

How could a mere bookseller live in such luxury? Especially one who seemed to sell so few books?

Men such as Mr. Foxe attract gossip. If it was wide of the mark, that was largely because the man himself did not offer to explain. From time to time, someone would come to the shop door of a morning, knock and be admitted at once. Since that someone would be a person of substance, it was widely believed that Mr. Foxe sold pornographic literature to the gentry. And if this was untrue – as indeed it was – Mr. Foxe made no effort to set the record straight.

That was how it was each morning, save only Sunday. Mr. Foxe left his house, sat for an hour or more in the coffee house, then took a turn along Gentleman's Walk and around the marketplace. On his way, he bowed or raised his hat to the many persons he knew, sometimes stopping to speak, though rarely for long. His walk would take him less than an hour, then he would return home to attend to business in his shop. Yet even that appeared to occupy little enough of his time, for the shop was rarely open to casual browsers for more than an hour or so in the afternoon. What he did with the rest of the day was a mystery. On Sundays he rarely left his house, for he was not a churchgoer and thus had little need to rouse himself. He might go out when the day had warmed enough to make walking in one of the city's gardens a pleasure. He might not be seen at all.

A quiet man, his friends said. A man with secrets, others countered. A man on the easiest of terms with everyone who mattered in the city, but on what basis no one quite knew. If he was rich, he didn't show it. If he was a person of influence, none knew whence that influence came. No mere bookseller, then. But what else he might be was so much a mystery that most simply accepted the enigma that was Ashmole Foxe and turned their attention to other matters.

The day when these events began was a Wednesday. A cool, blustery day when broad patches of blue sky betokened spring, but the wind itself remained wintry. During the night, it had rained a good deal, an event which pleased Mr. Foxe. His house, not far from St. Peter Mancroft Church, lay on the long slope down to the huge cathedral and the river beyond. The streets in this great city of Norwich resembled those in London itself, foul with mud, ordure and horse droppings. But today, the rain had washed much of this down the hill. That allowed Foxe to step out boldly. Since his shoes were expensive, he had no wish to cover them with mud if it could be avoided.

The events themselves began with a simple message. Since Foxe had left the coffee house and was making his way towards the marketplace, he must have received it sometime after eleven o'clock.

Feeling someone tug at his sleeve, Foxe looked down and saw an ill-dressed urchin with an uncommonly dirty face. The boy beckoned him to bend closer. Then he delivered his message in something between normal speech and a hoarse whisper. Since Foxe was above average height, and the urchin very small, this bending occasioned him some difficulty. Still he contrived to smile as he did it, hoping thus to reassure the diminutive person. Alfred often used young Charlie Dillon to carry messages. Foxe suspected the lad was tougher than he looked, but he had found kindness was often repaid in unexpected ways.

'Begging your pardon, Mr. Foxe, sir. Alfred do say as how you should come home directly. You has a visitor, he do say, and such as you will want to see right away.'

Straightening with some relief, Foxe took a penny from his purse. By now a grubby palm was already stretched out to receive it. Then, as the boy ran off, well pleased with his reward, Foxe turned towards St. Peter's Church and his home.

'It's Alderman Halloran. I put him in the parlour.' Alfred had let Foxe in through the shop door and was now speaking softly so that he should not be heard in the house beyond. Foxe nodded his head in response. It was no surprise that Alfred had summoned him at once. Alderman Benjamin Halloran was an important man in Norwich, a rich merchant, and one of Mr. Fox's best customers. It would not do to keep him waiting.

Foxe paused in the hallway to use the mirror. He straightened his wig slightly and checked that his stock was tied neatly. He liked to appear well-dressed when he could, as he liked to do all else well.

'Good morning, alderman. My apologies that I was not here to greet you. Have you been offered refreshments?'

The alderman showed the glass of punch he was holding. His solid frame, distinct paunch and rich attire marked him out at once for one of the wealthiest yarn merchants in a city renowned for its trade in fine worsted cloth.

'Morning, Foxe. I should apologise for coming unannounced. Alfred looked after me, as he always does. I've come straight here from talking with the mayor and some of my colleagues. We've got a difficult problem and your name came up.'

Foxe merely nodded. 'Will you take a seat, sir? I've a feeling you have a story to tell me.'

They sat either side of the fireplace. Foxe occupied his chair neatly, with his feet on the floor side-by-side. Alderman Halloran sprawled in his chair and stretched his legs out towards the hearth, though there was no fire at this time of year. His face was flushed and they were beads of dampness above his eyes. It must be a serious matter for him to have hastened so much.

'There's been a murder. Master Daniel Bonneviot. His family came from the Low Countries nigh on 150 years ago, but the name has stuck. Normally we let the family sort out finding the killer, but this Bonneviot was important. Important to the city, I mean. Besides, his wife is said to be something of a ninny and his only son has gone heaven knows where.'

Foxe waited.

'Damned fine workers, the Huguenots. Sober, industrious, highly skilled. They brought a great deal to this city. Of course, nearly all the present generation were born here. Still, they've generally kept to their forefathers' trade.'

'Weavers,' Foxe said.

'That's right. Calvinists, most of them. Prickly too.'

'I seem to recall ...' But Alderman Halloran wasn't listening.

'Much better than being Papists! I hope we'll be free of their kind now. Was it less than twenty years ago ... yes, 1745 ...' He was losing the thread of his story.

'The murder?'

The alderman shook himself. 'An important man, as I said. He'd done well. Bonneviot employed thirty or so weavers as out-workers. Worsted and damask. I've sold him yarns, on and off.'

'What was his secret?'

'Bonneviot was a hard man. He'd had to make his own way from weaver to employer. He had no time for those who wouldn't work as hard as he did.'

Now things were becoming clearer. Mr. Daniel Bonneviot was, it seemed, a noted master weaver in Norwich, who had done well for himself. Not quite one of the elite of the city – yet – but a rising star. Describing an employer as a hard man generally meant he demanded more than his workers wanted to give. A bully? Cruel to any who couldn't keep up?

Foxe didn't speak. Instead, he closed his eyes for a moment, then reopened them. Why come to him? The weavers formed their own community. It would be hard for any outsider to get them to talk.

'No one is quite sure who will take over the business. Maybe his son – he only has the one – maybe not. He and his father rarely saw eye-to-eye. He doesn't even live in the city, so far as I know.'

'How did he make his money. Bonneviot, I mean?"

'Norwich produces the finest worsted cloth in Britain. That makes us the ones to beat. We've plenty of competitors elsewhere and many are turning to new-fangled machinery to let them undercut our prices. Most of it's water-powered, so Norfolk isn't suitable for these manufactories, as they call them.'

'So they'll take our business?'

'If we let 'em! They can't come close to us in quality at present, but it's not every buyer who cares about that. Men like Bonneviot are vital. He employed a good many people. He cut costs harder than anyone and kept his trade when others lost theirs. And he had no time for all the restrictive working practices left over from the past.'

'None of which would make him popular.'

'There's the problem. This city is notorious for hotheads raising the rabble. The future for cloth trade is very uncertain, what with problems at home and wars abroad. Some have already lost their employment. More will follow them, if our weavers, dyers and other outworkers cling so stubbornly to their old ways. The fools blame anything and everyone else for taking their work. They never look at themselves. We're always sending constables in to break up various strikes and disturbances.'

The alderman drank all the rest of his punch in a single gulp. Foxe discreetly rose to fill his glass again, before returning to his seat.

'We can't afford to have problems like this now,' Alderman Halloran continued. 'Very bad for our trade in fine cloth. Very bad for the city. That's why the mayor sent me here. So far we're holding our own, but …'

'How may I assist His Worship?'

'This isn't a job for the constables. They're only fit to deal with vagabonds, whores, pickpockets and the like. We thought of asking someone to come from Bow Street in London, but they'd be far too conspicuous and none of the locals would speak to them anyway. Then your name came up.'

Foxe hadn't tasted his punch. Now he picked up the glass and took a delicate sip. Alfred had mixed it carefully and it tasted delicious.

'The job you did for us before was outstanding. I know this one will be tough but you're our best hope. We all agreed on that.'

What he meant was their last hope.

'Will you take it on? Will you help us as you have done before?'

Foxe waited for a few moments, then nodded. 'Please tell His Worship that I will do my best. I cannot, of course, guarantee success …'

'Good fellow!' The older man struggled to his feet, but as he turned towards the door, he paused.

'I don't suppose you've got anything for me? It's been a while …'

'At the moment, sir, I have not. However, I am conducting some delicate negotiations with a gentleman of great discernment who has temporally fallen on hard times due to gambling debts. It may be that in a few weeks …'

'Bear me in mind then. You know the kind of thing I like. We've done good business before, Foxe, as you know.'

'Indeed, Mr. Alderman. As I hope we will again. I will call Alfred to escort you out. I presume you came in via the shop?'

'Of course, Foxe. I know your habits.'

'Then Alfred will take you out that way. I will be in touch with you as soon as I have anything to report to the mayor.'

'Make it soon, Foxe, if you can. This situation could become very serious.'

'I will try, sir. Alfred, show the alderman out through the shop. A very good day to you, sir, and please give His Honour The Mayor my most sincere compliments.'

'Good day to you too, Foxe. Soon, remember! Both on the city's business and mine.'

Chapter Two

A Bookseller's Trade

IT WAS A MAGNIFICENT LIBRARY. There were shelves of books on every wall, running from floor to ceiling. The only gaps were the doors, the great fireplace and the four vast windows that let in enough daylight to read by. Since today the sun was shining, the shutters on these windows were part closed. The sixth and seventh earls had both insisted on it. Sunlight faded the leather bindings. Although the eighth earl was now the owner, he took no interest in the collection. The servants continued exactly as before. The seventh earl had only been dead these six months after all.

How many hours had the two previous earls spent in this room? How often had they taken favourite volumes from the shelves? How many times had their hands trembled in excitement as they unwrapped a fresh purchase?

Save for the servants, none came in now. To Foxe's keen eye, the books already seemed neglected, almost forlorn. He could see dust on the steps of the library ladder and on the top edges of the books in the lowest shelves. He half expected to be able to hear the steady noise of thousands of bookworms and silverfish chewing through the leaves in the largest folios. All that mattered now was the potential for raising cash. Soon all the best books would be gone. The seventh earl's appetite for gambling and enjoying himself must far outstrip the income from the estate. The best Foxe could do was rescue the cream of the collection and see them into the hands of kinder and more appreciative owners.

George, Eighth Earl of Pentelow, was not the 'gentleman of great discernment' Foxe had described to the alderman. That description applied to father and grandfather. The son who stood now in the library, gazing at the thousands of books his father and grandfather had bought, was a philistine. He could never see any attraction in musty, leather-bound tomes. If you had money and land enough, why bother with books? Money would buy you many more exciting pastimes. His grand house should, he had decided, become a perfect venue for balls, dinner parties and the gambling that went with them. Indeed, sweep away these wretched books and this massive room would make a perfect ballroom. He was happiest in London, of course, where he could enjoy the theatre, his many clubs and the many delights of the most wanton city in the land. If he had to come to Norfolk, at least he should have space to bring society to him. He had many friends who felt the same and lived close enough to visit and be visited. For the rest, gambling, drinking and wenching he could find anywhere.

Living by these beliefs, as eldest son, had already caused the shortage of ready cash that was obliging him to sell books. That link did not cross the eighth earl's mind.

'Look around, Foxe. My father spent hours in here, silly old fool. His father too. Well, at least they left me something to sell in hard times, I suppose. Take your pick. Only do not take too many. I would not have my visitors notice the shelves are emptier than they were. I can buy more books to fill up the spaces, you said?'

'I can find them for you, if you wish, my lord.'

'I do wish, Foxe. Can't see myself wandering around smelly bookshops and having to be polite to grubby booksellers. Ah, no offence intended, sir.'

'None taken, my lord. How much money are you looking to … raise?'

'Five hundred pounds, if it is possible.'

'Yes, that will demand some gaps, but not too many. Your esteem parent and his father were skilled collectors of many rare editions. I may be able to find that amount for you with a hundred books or less.'

'Capital, Foxe. I'll leave it to you then. Tell my footman which ones you want and he'll have them taken down and packed into boxes. Ah … no chance of swift payment, I expect? It's just that I have one or two rather pressing debts incurred at cards … '

'I will give you a banker's draft before I leave, my lord, if that is acceptable to you?'

'Acceptable? … You're a marvel, Foxe. Never cease to amaze me. Right, to work right away. I'll send someone with refreshments in a little while, shall I?'

'That would be most acceptable, my lord.'

As George, Eighth Earl of Pentelow, wandered off, Foxe mentally rubbed his hands with glee. To have access to a collection of this importance would bring him a great amount of profit. Better still, it would remove some of these priceless treasures from the hands of the spendthrift earl. Those who bought them would value them. They would also care for them better. The smell of old books charmed some people, but to Foxe it meant only one thing – decay.

Foxe wandered around for a while without any plan or direction. To tell the truth, he did not know where to begin. Amongst such riches he felt humbled. He was loath to turn to such a mundane task as picking out those most likely to find a ready buyer amongst his customers. Nor was there need to hurry. Unless the eighth earl mended his ways, which seemed unlikely, Foxe was sure he would return many times.

Now he roamed at random, taking down a volume from time to time to inspect it . Most he put back on the shelf. A select few he carried to the massive table in the middle of the room. There he set each down with the greatest care. To an onlooker, it might have appeared he thought them asleep and was trying not to awake them to what was happening. Foxe knew that in the sale of rare books, as in all kinds of art, condition was a major part of setting the price. His purchasers would seek out every tiny flaw or piece of damage in the hope of persuading him to accept less. It was his job to see they had no further source of bargaining than the ones already inflicted by age or neglect.

#

It was during this period of aimless wandering that Foxe noticed something odd about one of the bays of shelves. Or rather, something odd about the books it contained. For a start, they seemed too regular in size and binding. He knew many books were sold unbound, so that the purchaser could have them in personal bindings, often marked with a family crest. To have many books of the same height was also not unusual. After all, certain paper sizes were becoming standard, such as quartos and folios. But to have so many of such uniform width? That argued that all must contain almost the same number of pages, which he could not believe. He went over to look closer.

Here was another oddity. While each volume seemed similar in appearance, their subject-matter ranged over almost the whole gamut of topics. There were volumes of philosophy, history, theology, natural science, poetry and even the practice of agriculture. None seemed to be set in a series of volumes. And while most were in English, others were in Latin, French, Italian, Greek, Spanish and Dutch. All languages were muddled together. You might find a row that began with a work of philosophy in Latin, a book of Ancient Greek poetry next to it, then a treatise on navigation in French.

Foxe stood back and considered what this might mean. That it was deliberate, he was certain. On the other shelves he had browsed, someone had laid the volumes out in a clear and rigorous order. Might this bay consist only of books for whom no place might be found elsewhere? Single books in series, for which the other volumes were missing? Bound groups of pamphlets or the like? But would not such a miscellany always contain items of many different sizes and lengths? How would it produce the suspicious uniformity which had drawn his attention in the first place?

Idly, he drew first one book from the nearest shelf, then several more. Another mystery! Not only were these volumes alike in every dimension and detail of binding. All had pages of an odd shape. The height was consistent with quarto size, but it seemed that all the leaves must be no more than four inches width! It was as if each book had been sliced in half from top to bottom. Thus it would fit shelves of maybe half the depth of a normal shelf for books of this size.

Foxe took one of the books in his hand and sought out several similar-looking books on other shelves. He was right! Lay one book on top of the other and the two would be almost the same height. Look at the width and one was barely half as wide as the other. These shelves had been made expressly for this library. It must be deliberate that one bay was far shallower than all the others. As in most great libraries, the largest volumes were in shelves close to the floor. These were both taller and deeper that the others, so that they could accommodate the great size of the books in them. Then came a kind of shelf, formed by the top of these deeper shelves meeting shallower shelving above them. From here to the ceiling, the shelves were uniform in height and depth. Smaller books were placed in line with the rest, leaving a gap behind them.

All except the shelves in that one bay. Here both the dimensions of the shelves and of the books were of near total regularity.

Perhaps there was some reason why shelves of more normal dimension could not be made here? A chimney breast from an older part of the building? Even a priest's hole, though such were rare in Norfolk. It had long been a most protestant area and supplied many for the Parliamentarian armies in the Civil War against the first Charles. Still, it might be possible. Where better to hide an entrance than behind a bay of bookshelves in a vast library?

'Priest's hole?' The Earl said. 'Not to my knowledge. Anyhow, that part of the house was only built in my grandfather's time. Not much need for priest's holes then, I would have thought. And there's nothing behind that wall either, except a passageway used by the servants.'

'You never heard of some hidden cupboard or the like?'

'Never. Of course, I didn't go into the library that much. Not my kind of place. But I'm sure I would have known of anything like that.'

'So you won't know how it might open, assuming there is anything to open?'

'No idea! Grub around, Foxe. You're a curious kind of fellow. If there's a hoard of hidden treasure, I'll rely on you to find it. By God, I could do with treasure right now. D'you think you'll be able to raise the cash I need?'

'I have little doubt of it, my lord. I must contact potential purchasers, of course. They will wish to bargain, which takes some time. Yet they will hand over their money in the end.'

'It's all so confounded slow!'

'Indeed, my lord. I cannot rush these things, if you are to obtain the best prices. Nor can I walk through a library such as yours and pull books from the shelves as if they were bags of tea. I will need to return, perhaps several times, before I can be certain of fulfilling your request in the best and least obvious way.'

His lordship would have protested again at the delay this must cause, but Foxe forestalled him. 'I believe that you have some temporary embarrassment that is pressing, my lord. Is that not so?'

'Most pressing, Foxe!'

'Then I may be able to help. I have prepared a banker's draft for two hundred pounds. I have it here. Will that be of use?'

'Of use? Of use? It will save my life and reputation, Foxe! I knew I could rely on you. Come as often as you like. No need to wait upon me being at home. I will give the servants orders to admit you to the library at any time you wish.'

'I have left perhaps a dozen volumes on the large table in the centre of the library, my lord. Your footman has my instructions on how they should be packed and sent to my shop. It is most important that he follows them to the letter. To damage a book is to lessen its value in that instant.'

'I'll make damn sure he treats them like the most delicate china! All will be done as you wish. I will have them transported in my own carriage for additional safety.'

'Then, my lord, with your permission I will take my leave.'

The earl's coach was summoned, Foxe was brought his coat and hat, and the two men took their leave of one another. As Foxe travelled back to Norwich, most of his thoughts remained in the earl's library, puzzling over the nature of that single bay and its contents.

Chapter Three

Friends and Lovers

THE LAND BEHIND MR. FOX's house was surrounded by a high wall, which he kept in excellent repair. The only way through it was via a strong pair of wooden carriage gates, always secured by a heavy beam within. The small door set into the right-hand gate, however, was usually unlocked during the day. It provided entrance or exit to the tradesmen who came to collect orders, and the draymen who brought deliveries. Mrs. Dobbins, Mr. Fox's cook and housekeeper, was known to be a good customer. She also had sharp eyes for any attempt to provide light weight or less than the best quality. Since she paid fair rates for what she needed, and her employer paid his bills promptly – which was quite a novelty – those eyes were rarely needed. All who did business with the house made sure not to put such important custom at risk.

The space behind this wall was taken up by a substantial coachhouse with stables and tack-room attached. None were in use at present. Within the city, Foxe preferred to walk or hire a chair. On his various journeys, he used the stage or obtained a suitable conveyance and driver from a local inn. He was well aware that his style of life already drew comment. It was unthinkable that a mere bookseller should own a coach and horses and employ the groom and coachman to go with them. So, though he could well afford such luxuries, he chose to avoid the curiosity they would bring with them.

Anyone passing by that day might have seen a man leaving by the entrance to the coachhouse and yard. That he was a tradesman was clear by his clothing. A baker or a shopkeeper from elsewhere in the city come to collect payment for his latest account.

The man did not hurry. Once or twice he paused for a moment, as if unsure of his way, for he looked around him carefully before going on. At length he came to the marketplace. There he walked with greater assurance, slipping easily between the mass of stalls and customers as if he was now on known ground.

To one side of the marketplace lay a maze of narrow streets, lined by shops and houses. There the ground fell away towards the quays and warehouses along the riverside. The Lanes, people called them. They often contained the homes and businesses of tradesmen and artisans like this man. Perhaps he lived there, for he seemed to know his way well.

Coming to an inn, he slipped inside and waved to the landlord with the assurance of a regular customer.

'Is Brock here?' he asked.

'As always. You do know where to find him. I'll send Molly over with more ale.'

Indeed, Brock was in his usual place, an empty pot of ale before him. His eyes were shut and he seemed to be asleep. Yet, when the new arrival was still more than two yards distant, he greeted him, his voice made harsh by too much tobacco and too many years on the river.

'Foxe,' he said, without bothering to open his eyes. 'Thought you'd be here soon. Molly bringing ale?'

'Have no fear. She'll be with us shortly, though I dare say you've taken some already. Now, there's something I need your help to deal with …'

'Master Bonneviot's murder, I'll wager.'

'Then you would win. Tell me what you know, Brock. Softly, mind. I would not have the world hear what we are talking about.'

'Wouldn't matter,' Brock said. 'Everyone's talking about the same thing. Found in an alley close to Colegate with 'is throat cut.'

'Robbed?'

'Maybe. If he were, it wouldn't have been much. Too wise a cove to go about in this city with more than a few coins in his purse. The word is he were 'sassinated.'

'Any idea why?'

'He were a hard man.' There was that phrase again. 'Not too popular with his workers or those who supplied him with yarn and the like. He always drove a hard bargain, then only paid when 'e had too.'

'Why do business with him, then?'

'People couldn't afford not to. He might have been rough to work for, but the work he gave was steady. If you were good, he paid as well as anyone else. If you weren't, he laid you off. Simple.'

'Cruel.'

'Not by his way o' thinking. He'd 'ad to work and scrape a living at the start, so 'e never saw why others should 'ave things too easy.'

The girl brought their ale, placing the pitcher in front of Brock, with an extra cup for Mr. Foxe. She smiled at the two men, then winked at Foxe and threw a quick glance towards the staircase. He smiled back, but shook his head.

'Busy. But thank you.'

'She'll get you up there one day, I warrant,' Brock said as she left. 'Pretty enough, even for the likes o' you, Foxe. Good tits on 'er too.'

'Drink your ale, Brock. Will you help me again? Same as before?'

'Aye. I reckoned that were what you came for. Already decided before you walked through that door.'

'So. Tell me what you know of Bonneviot. What about his business, for example?'

'Not doin' too well is the word about 'ere. Lots of different notions of why. These are good times for cloth merchants and weavers in this city. The most likely tale is that he fell into some quarrel with the Londoners who buy most of what 'e made. That may 'ave lowered 'is sales for the moment.'

'Any speculation about his death?'

'Plenty! Some says it was just some cut-purse: a robbery gone wrong. Others reckon 'e 'ad it coming to 'im for years. Always falling out with someone, Bonneviot. If it's right that he wasn't paying his accounts too readily at present, someone might 'ave decided to get 'is own back.'

'Not a good reason for murder, Brock. Kill your debtor and you'll never see your bill paid.'

'Could 'ave been some weaver or servant he'd treated bad. Bonneviot wasn't a man to treat anyone well. If someone 'ad annoyed 'im, he might well 'ave served 'em some slight or harm.'

'Maybe. Maybe.'

'You ain't convinced.'

'No. Do we know what he was doing in that part of the city?'

'No idea. Still, there's no reason he shouldn't 'ave been there. A good many well-off merchants 'as homes in Colegate. He could've been going to visit a friend – if he 'ad any – or a woman. You never sees 'is wife.'

'Children?'

'A daughter by 'is first wife and one son by the second. Not much known of late about the lad. Hasn't been seen in the city for a good few years. Said to be inclined in the artistic way … and y'know what folks mean by that!'

'Are they right?'

'Maybe. I suspect he 'ad a hard upbringing. Do as you're told and like it. One or two who knew the family well says that, in time, the boy turned against 'is father. Argued with 'im over just about everything, then took off sayin' he was going' on the stage. Mind, with a father like that, you'd either grow up just as nasty or turn into a molly.'

'So, what's the son like?'

'Smallish, thin, a bit limp-looking. Mother spoiled him and his father despised him.'

'Know where he is?'

'No idea.'

'Not following his father's trade, by what you said.'

'Don't take all that stuff about goin' on the stage too serious. Many a lad rows with 'is father round about that same age. Mostly they sorts it out. Bonneviot did 'is apprenticeship in London. His son might be doin' the same.'

Foxe downed his second cup of ale and stood up. 'I'll drop in again in a day or so. If you get anything more before, send word by Charlie Dillon. He knows where to find me.'

'Clever little scrap, Charlie, for all he's a runt. Not surprising, mind you. His ma's always in and out of the workhouse or in and out of gaol. Must be hard to be a whore's kid. I gives 'im a few pennies when I can.'

'I do too,' Foxe said, 'and, I'll bet, a good many other men who're sorry for him. I wouldn't be surprised if he earns more than you do some days.'

'Doubt it. I'm may be too old for honest work, but I have others to work for me.'

'Indeed you do,' Foxe said. 'Now, where did Bonneviot live?'

'Round about Cow Tower way. Cross the river and you'll find the house on the left. Not too far from 'is warehouses along the river.'

'I thought I might talk to some of his weavers.'

'Will they talk to you?'

'Only one way to find out. Now, get to business, Brock,' Foxe said. 'Find out whatever else you can. Don't spend your time and money in here downing ale and ogling poor little Molly.'

'Poor little Molly? She'd service both of us within the space of half an hour, then go back to serving ale without another thought.'

'You may be right.'

'I know I'm right. I likes young Molly, but I ain't blind to how she makes most of her money. Now, if you want to know all about what rich folk like Bonneviot get up to in their spare time, go and see Gracie Catt.'

'How do you know that's where I'm going next?'

'It's where I'd go. Leave me in peace to get on with finding out what I can.'

'Very well, Brock. Here, give Molly this shilling from me before you leave.'

'For what? Smiling at you? Give it to 'er yourself and I warrant you'll get a least a kiss – and probably a moment or two before she pushes your 'and away.'

'No, I'm in a hurry. You can have the kiss in my place.'

'Got expectations with Mistress Gracie, 'as you?' But Foxe was gone.

By now, Foxe reckoned it would be about the right time to call on Mistress Gracie Catt. It was late enough for her to be out of bed, but early enough for her establishment to be entertaining few clients. First, he must return home to change his clothes.

Once again, he slipped in through the back gate. When he came out, he was unrecognisable. It was clear this man was a foreigner and more than a little of the dandy. Yet he could not be a gentleman. No, he was bound for work of some superior kind, perhaps as a music tutor or singing master. He carried a portfolio beneath his arm and, as he walked, beat time with the other and hummed to himself.

A large man, looking somewhat foolish in footman's garb, opened the door to Mistress Catt's house. It would not have been wise, however, to cross him. Fortunately, he seemed to know Foxe, nodding an acknowledgement and stepping back to allow the visitor to move inside.

'Signor Vulpino.'

'Horton. Is your mistress ready to receive visitors?'

'I believe so, signor. Wait 'ere and I'll find out.'

A few moments later, the man returned and beckoned to Foxe. 'You knows the way, signor. She's waiting in her boudoir for you.'

Mr. Foxe – or Signor Vulpino, teacher of deportment, as most knew him here – walked upstairs and along a lengthy corridor. There he encountered several of Mistress Catt's ladies and received many kisses. All were delighted to see him. A girl who looked good and moved like a lady could command a higher price for her favours. If she became truly elegant in appearance and manner, she might even reach a point where she could choose her clients herself. Higher still and she could hope one of the gentlemen might wish her to be his exclusive property. To become the mistress of a rich man, who would set them up in their own accommodation and load them with jewels and dresses, was the ultimate ambition.

Mistress Catt waited until Signor Vulpino had made his bow, then rose and spoke to the maid who waited just outside her door.

'No interruptions after you've brought tea, Sally.'

Then she turned to her visitor with a practiced and professional smile. 'I am delighted you have come, Signor Vulpino. Please take a seat. One of my newest girls, straight from a village, is in sore need of your professional help. For a few weeks, I can manage to present her as an unsullied virgin. But even my customers soon remember they've either deflowered her already or know someone who has.'

'How old is she, Mistress Grace?'

'Fifteen. Well-developed for her age, but yet childlike enough to pass for an innocent.'

'I will be delighted to assist her, signora. And your other ladies?'

'All would benefit from some extra tuition.'

The two of them went on in this vein until tea had been brought and Sally closed the door behind her as she left.

Foxe enjoyed a lengthy gaze at the woman before him. En déshabillé, she looked ravishing, from her rich, dark curls to her neat feet in their silken slippers. Sadly, ravishment would have to wait. He still had another call to make this afternoon.

'Business or pleasure, Ashmole?' Mistress Catt asked.

'Unfortunately, business.'

'I hope you do not favour my sister above me, sir.'

'Never, Gracie, my dear. As you know, I am most careful to give neither of you cause for jealousy.'

'The mayor has asked you to investigate Bonneviot's murder?'

How did she know? The same way she knew everything else.

'Indeed. Can you instruct your ladies, please? On the usual terms, I suggest.'

'A little on account?'

Foxe leaned across and kissed her. A long, slow kiss compounded of equal parts desire and affection. When he straightened up, he opened the portfolio he had brought with him. From it he withdrew a small purse, which he dropped into Gracie's open palm.

'You know kissing me like that makes me want more,' Gracie said.

As the madam of the most fashionable and expensive bordello in Norwich, Gracie Catt no longer needed to work on her own account. However, being but 30 years of age, she was still in her prime and had no intention of wasting it. The next time he came, he had better be in condition. Gracie both expected and gave the highest levels of performance.

'Business?' Foxe asked in a soft tone.

'Business.'

'Was Bonneviot a customer?'

Did he notice a distinct shudder before she answered?

'Once or twice. Then I barred him.'

'The reason?'

There it was again.

'He was … quite rough. I care for my girls, Ash. I won't have them mistreated. We have several customers who enjoy certain … special services. Some girls are happy to oblige, for an extra fee, of course. I force none to do so. Bonneviot said nothing in advance, then caused … injuries. The first time I warned him. The second time, I had Horton throw him into the street. He never came back.'

'His son?'

'Hah! Came once, but couldn't get the job done, despite all the help my girls gave him. He's a feeble specimen, Ash. Makes a lot of noise to hide the fact he can't get it up. Might do better with a boy, of course.'

'You think so?'

'Who knows?'

Foxe pondered a moment.

'Get many of the other Master Weavers here, Gracie?'

'Quite a few.'

'They're the target then. What did they think of Bonneviot? How did he treat his business rivals? Was he doing well, or beginning to slip?'

Gracie inclined her head in agreement. She knew that would cause him acute discomfort. He had to bite the inside of his cheek hard to stop himself jumping up and covering that long, beautiful neck with kisses.

'Sorry, Gracie. I really do have to go. I need to talk to your sister before she starts getting ready for this evening's performance.'

'You know she'll tell me if you …'

'I know. Merciful God! How you two work on me! Oh, my poor heart …'

Gracie laughed in a most unladylike way. 'I've heard it said some people wear their heart on their sleeve, Ash. This is the first time I've met someone who wears his heart tucked in the front of his breeches!'

Foxe snatched up his portfolio and fled before his resolve crumbled altogether.

'Have you been to my sister?'

Miss Catherine Catt – Kitty on the stage – was two years her sister's junior with rich, auburn hair and the temper to match. Apart from that, the sisters closely resembled each other. Gracie was a little taller, a brown-eyed brunette with a slightly fuller figure. Kitty was more delicate and elfin-looking and had startling green eyes. Their father, Edward Catt, had been a prosperous local merchant who fell for the ravishing Peggie Lewisham, burlesque actress and dancer. She had given their two daughters her beauty. Their father had contributed both his brains and his business sense. The women's morals were entirely their own choice.

Foxe nodded.

'Did you …?'

He sighed. "No, Kitty. I'm sure you'll ask her to be sure, but the answer is still no. I am well aware that it's your turn next.'

'One day, Ash, we'll maybe meet you together.'

'God in heaven, you'd need to give me warning! I can just about manage each of you alone. Together would be enough to put an end to me.'

'But what a way to go!'

'Stop it, Kitty! I've already had to fight your sister off. It's too much to expect me to go through that all again. Look, to be fair, I'll give you exactly what she extorted from me.'

The same long kiss, then a swift withdrawal, just in time to prevent Kitty's hand from completing its journey to his groin.

'This is business, Kitty. Behave!'

'I am behaving.'

'Badly! Now put your delightful little claws away, Kitty dear, and stop tormenting me.'

Sometimes he wondered why he subjected himself to their constant teasing. Was it just their beauty and eagerness for …? With Kitty so close he didn't dare use the word, even to himself. Well, that was a good part of it, if he was being honest. Yet there was more. Both were uncommonly intelligent. Both were bold. Both were damn good actresses, even if one worked on a somewhat smaller and more intimate stage – or used to.

'So, Ash. Business. Who am I to be this time?'

'Don't know yet, Kitty. I'm sure you know by now the mayor has asked me to look at Daniel Bonneviot's murder.'

'I didn't, but I'm not surprised.'

Kitty didn't have the same access to information as her sister, it appeared. That didn't matter to Foxe, since he employed Kitty in quite a different capacity.

'Yes … well, I'm going to need to talk to one or two of his close family members. I thought maybe we could revive one of our couples. You can be my beautiful young wife. I can be your rich but sour husband.'

Kitty clapped her hands. 'Even better, we could attend to offer our condolences. You provide a manly shoulder for the widow to cry upon and I console the menfolk.'

'Kitty! That is enough! If you won't play properly, I won't let you play at all.'

He was rewarded with a sullen pout and a sharp rap on the knee.

'It may not even be those characters. I know almost nothing about the family at this point. The little I do know suggests that Bonneviot kept them all on a short rein, especially in terms of money. The son, I've been told, went to London to go on the stage.'

'Bonneviot … might use a different stage name, of course … no, never heard of him.'

'I can't claim to be surprised. Your sister described him as a feeble object. It seems even her girls couldn't coax a rise out of him, if you understand me.'

'Pah! I don't want to go near him then. Is he a molly?'

'Nobody I have spoken to seems to know. But that's beside the point for the moment. All I need from you today, my dear, is your assurance that you will help me, on the usual terms.'

'All …?'

'Catherine Catt! You are, I declare, a thoroughly shameless baggage!'

'That's why you love me, Ash.'

'Alas, you are correct – at least in part. I also think you are beautiful, clever, bold and an extremely talented actress. You could be a star of the London stage, if only you could rouse yourself ...'

'Truce! Truce! If you go through all that again, I will scream. Apart from the beautiful, bold, clever and talented bit, of course. You can play that tune as often as you like. Very well, dearest Ash. I will assist you again, as you always knew I would.

Now be off with you. I am playing the lead tonight and must prepare myself without unnecessary distractions.'

'Oh,' Foxe said. 'That's what you call it, is it?'

As he left, in some haste, Miss Kitty Catt's hairbrush struck the door behind him, right where his head might have been. Thus, as he descended to the street, he mentally added accuracy in throwing to her many other talents.

Chapter Four

By the River

AT THIS STAGE, MR. FOXE needed most to see and feel how the dead man and those around him lived. He always did this at the start of any investigation. It was impossible to understand things otherwise. Nor could he frame the right questions until he could set them against the appropriate background.

That's why, the next morning, Mr. Foxe the bookseller missed his normal morning coffee for once. Instead, he slipped out of the house and walked away towards the river.

The great city of Norwich was still enclosed, in large part, by its old city walls. These had such a large circuit that moving beyond them had not yet become necessary enough to change the city's shape. Here in the northern quadrant, across the River Wensum, a district had grown up between the water and the walls. A distinctive neighbourhood, in many ways, and one devoted to weaving, spinning and the textile trade.

Starting in the days of Queen Elizabeth, a flood of Protestant refugees had left the Low Countries. For almost a hundred years, religious persecution drove them out. France, Spain and Austria fought over the lands they held. Who won mattered little. To these Catholic monarchs, so many Protestants would always be unacceptable.

The refugees scattered to the few Protestant countries open to them. Many settled in England, where most found London to their liking. Of those who moved on again, a majority favoured Norwich, England's second city.

Relations with these immigrants, known as Strangers, were not always easy. Yet Norfolk already had long ties with the other shores of the German Ocean. A few generations saw the vast majority of Strangers mix into the local population and lose their distinct culture.

One of their remaining legacies to Norwich was this district just to the north of the river. Many of the Strangers had worked in the great cloth trades of Flanders. Their skills and industry had helped to lift Norwich to its present position as the premier place in England for the production and finishing of fine worsteds.

Foxe did not hurry. It was a fine day and he enjoyed the sights and sounds of the city along the way. To a visitor, buildings and streets would seem little different to those of any other great city, save in one thing: the scarcity of people abroad.

There was plenty of activity along the river though. Gangs of men loading or unloading barges and wherries. Carters moving between the warehouses which lined the quays. Shouts from within the boats' holds and from those lined up to fetch and carry.

Foxe wandered along the quay amongst all the hustle and bustle. At first sight, you would have thought him indifferent to his surroundings. Yet he always seemed able to anticipate an obstruction and step aside in good time. In reality, he was drinking it all in. The cacophony of noises. The boats' hulls banging against the quays. The heavy steps of the dockers. The creaking of wood and rope. The constant murmur of voices – now punctuated by a shout or a curse – mixed with the shrill yelping of the gulls. And the smells! Tar, hemp, wood, the stained water of the river, the sweat of those heaving on ropes or lifting sacks and bales. Even the cargoes added scents as you passed. Here was grain or malt going to Yarmouth to be shipped to London or overseas. There was coal for the city's fires. Here teas, or spices, or bricks, or the roof tiles the Dutch boats used for ballast.

After he crossed the bridge, he turned to the right, towards the Cow Tower. That was where he recalled that Brock had said Daniel Bonneviot's house lay. The street now angled away from the water, leaving a space filled by warehouses. All had one side open to the boats and the quays and the other to the street to provide entry to carts.

The sounds and scents changed also. Here was the clue to why Norwich's streets often seemed oddly empty of people. This was a working city. From windows high in many of the houses came the constant slap and clatter of the weavers' looms. As you passed by others, you could hear the low, rhythmic humming of spinning wheels. Along the quays, people worked and talked in the open air. Here the workers stayed hidden within. For long days – even for some nights too – they attended to the production of what were known as 'Norwich stuffs'. The fine, glossy fabrics that were the city's pride and its main source of income.

Foxe looked for an urchin. There would always be some about. Such children would be too young to work yet – which meant very young indeed. Instead they spent their time running errands, picking pockets, or playing in the streets and gutters. Their mothers and elder sisters worked at their spinning wheels. Their older brothers sat at the drawlooms in the garrets, pulling up the warp threads while their fathers threw the weft shuttle.

Finding such an urchin, Foxe enquired which was Bonneviot's house.

'You be too late, mister. T'others be there afore you, already beatin' on the door. An that won't do 'em no good. That's a hard man, that Bonneviot is. No wonder that's got 'is throat cut, as I 'eard. A wonder 'e wasn't killed long afore this.'

'What others? There's a penny for a smart lad with the right answer.'

'Don't know who. But they be plenty riled up. A big group on 'em. Summat about bein' cheated out of what's rightfully theirs. Look! 'Ere they comes now. I told 'e they'd get nothin' from that place.'

A group of perhaps six or eight men was approaching.

'Be that good enough for my penny, mister?'

Foxe paid up. He would go to look at Bonneviot's house another time. Now he waited until the group passed him, all exchanging angry remarks and yelling curses over their shoulders towards the place they had just left. Then he wandered along behind them, not too close, but good enough to see where they went.

As Foxe expected, the group went no further than a tavern some fifty yards or so from the bridge he had just crossed. For a while, he waited outside, lounging against a wall, until he judged they would be well enough settled with jugs of ale. Then he went within, ducking his head under the lintel and finding the level of noise even greater than he had expected. Indeed, he had almost to shout to the landlord in his stained and greasy apron, just now returning behind his bar, for his own pot of ale.

'What's all the fuss about?' he asked.

'No bloody idea,' the landlord said. 'They ain't none of our regulars. If they thinks they can drown their sorrows in my ale, then wreck the place to work off their anger, they thinks wrong.'

He slid one hand under the counter and brought it up again, now wrapped around a fearsome wooden truncheon.

'I should keep away from 'em, mister. Sit you over there in the corner. They'll neither see nor bother you there. I can see at once you ain't the disputatious type.'

Foxe followed the landlord's advice. It was what he was going to do anyway. He'd be close enough there to hear what was going on, especially if they kept shouting as loudly as they were.

'Bastard owed me nigh on five pounds! Who's going' to pay now, that's what I wants to know. I got childer to feed.'

'We all be in the same boat. Bonneviot owed me a tidy sum too. Kept pressin' me to work faster and longer hours, then tries to cheat me out of the few shillin' he agreed to pay.'

'Someone did for 'im though, din't they. 'E got what 'e deserved. I hopes that's black soul do go right to 'ell. That's where 'e ought to be.'

'Course, now that's dead, who'll pay anyhow? It'll all be talk o' wills and lawyers. More delaying while poor men starves.'

'An' 'e weren't the only one in this city playing suchlike tricks on 'onest working men! All they masters be at the same game. As soon as they got any excuse, they lays us off. 'Ow can we live like that, that's what I wants to know.'

'I say we comes back o'night and brings a few torches. Lobs 'em through 'is winders.'

'Them bastard constables 'ud be on us afore we even got there, I reckon. Old mayor an' 'is cronies be runnin' scared o' summin' like that. This 'ole place be full o' constables after dark.'

'I did see some fair flints in the street back there. Couldn't we slip back and lob a few o' them beauties through 'is glassworks right now?'

This suggestion met with general agreement and some rapid downing of the remaining ale. Foxe slipped away before the others left. He wanted to be well clear before any trouble broke out. Besides, he'd learned a good deal of what he wanted to know. Maybe, if he hurried, he could fill in a few more blanks before it was time for dinner.

The trouble with visiting all parts of the city, Foxe decided, was all the costume changes it demanded. You had to blend in sufficiently, or no one would speak a word in your presence. Without that, he could have gone at once to his next potential information source. But it would never do to arrive at Alderman Halloran's home dressed as he was and expect to gain admittance.

Back home then. A word with Alfred to summon a chair. Foxe did not want the world and his wife to notice where he was going. A swift change into attire more suitable for the elegant and urbane bookseller visiting a rich customer. A wig and hat to top it all off. Then a few moments working out the questions he needed to ask, before the chair arrived.

All this, of course, depended on Halloran being at home. There might be a meeting of the City Council. He would take that chance.

Foxe sat well back in the chair to shield himself from the casual watcher and thought hard during the short trip to the alderman's house.

What had Bonneviot been up to? As one of the master weavers in a city devoted to the cloth trade, he should be more than usually prosperous. Hadn't Halloran said Bonneviot employed about thirty weavers. That was well above the usual number, so it marked him out as particularly successful.

A hard man. Would that alone account for him delaying payments to his workers? The habitual urge to demand quick payment and pay tardily? Foxe knew relations between the great men of the city and the thousands of self-employed workers were tense. The weavers, dyers, hot pressers and finishers, who produced the great bales of finished cloth sent to the London buyers, felt they didn't get a fair share of the profits. That was why the people of Norfolk, and especially Norwich, had a reputation for being turbulent and fractious.

Someone had murdered Bonneviot. Had some angry worker come upon him, demanded his money and, being pushed aside, drawn a knife and killed his tormentor? Was it as simple as that? Or was this death planned and thought through in advance?

Foxe's luck was good. The alderman's footman invited him inside, took his hat and stick and said he would ask his master if he was available to speak with a visitor. When he returned, he led the way into a pleasant parlour room where Halloran was waiting.

'Surprised to see you so soon, Foxe. Solved it all?'

'Not yet, Alderman. I have made one or two discoveries, however, that have raised questions I hope you can answer. At this stage, I would like to be sure I am at least on the right track.'

'Glad to see you so busy. Mr. Mayor has already been bothering me for news. I gather his informants are telling him there may be some move to attack the premises of the city's master weavers. Quite a few men have been laid off in the past few weeks. Being hungry and without work brings a powerful urge to hit out at someone.'

'That's one of my questions, alderman. I thought our cloth trade was healthy. Yet this implies some master weavers at least have less business that they once did.'

'What you have to understand, Foxe, is that the trade has constants ups and downs. The men in London who buy our cloth are prey to people's whims. One minute, fine satin is all the rage in the capital. The next it's muslin or damasks. Then only silk will do – or camlacoes or camblets. And that's without reckoning on the ups and downs in people's wealth or willingness to buy. About the only trade that's steady is bombazine for mourning dresses.'

'A difficult trade overall, then.'

'And one in the hands of those same London merchants. The weavers and merchants of Halifax have long sold much of their produce abroad. There demand may be rising, even as home demand is falling. Thus it evens out.'

'Do our master weavers not sell abroad too, sir?'

'Most certainly. But almost always through those same London dealers. To trade overseas requires a good deal of capital, which our men lack. Prices may be good, but you may wait long for payment. Meanwhile, you have to meet your own costs.'

'Ah, now I see, sir. But that would apply to the whole of the Norfolk cloth trade, wouldn't it?'

'Yes it would, Foxe. But these new manufactories in the north of the country use machines, even if the quality suffers. That means their costs are lower than ours. We still use independent workers in their own homes. We can only survive by cutting our costs to the bone in hard times. That means low wages and people paid off.'

'So if Bonneviot did this, he wouldn't be acting unusually for a Norwich master weaver?'

'Ah, Bonneviot. A hard man, as I said before. No, everyone has to lay people off sometimes. But Bonneviot … Bonneviot cut hard and he cut fast. Most of us don't like putting good men out of work. We try to wait fashion out or reduce costs in other ways first. Not Bonneviot. At the first sniff of weak trade, out they went. People reckoned he enjoyed showing how powerful he was.'

'So why work for him?'

'Simple. He was the largest single employer – or one of the largest. Besides, if you complained or failed to turn up when he needed you, you wouldn't work for him again. In some cases, so the stories go, he even put false rumours about of thieving so no other master would take the man on either.'

'Another question, alderman, if I may. You told me the other day you had sold him yarn. But you implied you'd only done it from time to time. I think those were your exact words.'

'Bonneviot didn't like to pay even a quarter as much as he liked to collect payments due to him. He'd find reasons to delay, or complain about the quality, or simply say he'd forgotten. However he did it, you'd find yourself waiting for months for him to settle your account. My business is large enough to be able to avoid customers like that. Others weren't so fortunate.'

Foxe thanked the alderman for being so helpful and rose to take his leave.

'A word, sir. I would send a few constables to patrol the area beyond the river for the next few nights. I think various people have grudges they want to settle by attacking Bonneviot's house and warehouse.'

'How the devil did you know that! Word reached me only moments before you arrived that some rabble had been throwing stones at his house this very day. Already sent someone to call the constables and make sure they're alert for worse. I'm glad I did, now you've mentioned it too.'

'Oh, and one last thing. I think I may have one or two things for your personal attention soon.'

'Good, Foxe, good. Just send word and I'll be round. Damn me! You move fast when you've a mind to it.'

As Foxe returned to the chair waiting for him outside, he was well pleased with his day. Bonneviot had indeed been a hard man. The question was, how else might he have sought his own profit at others' expense?

Back home again, Foxe planned his next moves. There was so much he needed to know. Brock had yet to come to him with news and Gracie Catt's girls were not yet likely to have much to tell him. They were well used to getting information from their clients, but the men in bed with them would have other things on their minds than Bonneviot's murder.

No, it was up to him. Those assisting him would do what they could, but the problems were for him to solve, not them.

Calling Alfred, he asked him to find the boy, Charlie Dillon, and tell him to be ready to carry a message to Kitty Catt, either at her house or at the Theatre Royal. Then he prepared to word his note carefully. Would dear Kitty please send word to her many theatrical contacts in London to enquire after the Bonneviot son? He did not know his first name, but such a distinctive surname should suffice. Was he working on the stage? What was known of him?

Kitty and her sister rarely did anything without expecting some reward. He therefore added mention of a grand ball that he had heard would be held at Thomas Ivory's new Assembly House the next month. If he was pleased with her, he wrote, he might ask her to accompany him. That should do it.

The note was written and thrust into Charlie's dirty hand, together with three whole pence for his trouble. Then Foxe returned to his tasks for the next two days.

First, he decided, he would visit the Calderwood sisters, Hannah and Abigail. Once they had run a Dame School for the children of those who could afford the penny each day they charged per child. Many sent their children largely to know they were safe while their parents worked. Nonetheless, the sisters taught all to read and most to write enough for their future needs. Boys they taught simple arithmetic. Girls learned sewing to make clothes for themselves and their families.

Best of all, these two ladies, who must both be beyond their seventieth year, had lived amongst the working people of Norwich their whole lives. If anyone could tell him the story of Daniel Bonneviot's life and background, it would be them.

Bonneviot's financial status also worried him. For the past few years, Norwich master weavers had been riding high. The worsteds, camblets and other materials they produced, were in strong demand. Norfolk shawls had never been more popular. Whether it was silk and camblet for petticoats or flowered and patterned stuff for a gentleman's waistcoat, London wanted what Norwich provided.

Why, then, had Bonneviot been laying weavers off? Why had he been seeking to drive his costs down so much? There was a mystery there and one that might have a good deal to do with his death.

Yet how to discover the answer was a problem. In the end, Foxe decided on a double approach. He would see if he could start a useful conversation amongst the denizens of the coffee-house. All would have known Bonneviot and many might have done business with him. Then he would visit his friend and customer Mr. Nathan Hubbard. Hubbard was an attorney much involved in drawing up contracts, leases and bills of sale. He was also an inveterate gossip with a nose for future business. If Bonneviot were in financial trouble, Hubbard might sense a chance for profitable legal work.

So far so good. What else? Yes, Sebastian Hirons.

The Norfolk Intelligencer was one of the more useful newspapers in the city. Mr. Sebastian Hirons was its editor. Editions came out thrice weekly, carrying London, national and international news as well as information on local matters. Since a city devoted to trade, banking and shipping, as Norwich was, had a great need for accurate, up-to-date news, Hirons was a man who knew many things. He also had a prodigious memory. Many times, articles in his paper drew links between events past and present in a way that other papers could not match. Foxe had known him for many years. There had once been few boundaries between printers, booksellers, and the publishers of broadsides and newspapers. Mr. Fox's own father had been a printer of broadsides, corantos, pamphlets, handbills and other forms of street news-sheets.

Now, he must talk with Bonneviot's widow. Everyone had ignored her. The alderman had called her a ninny. Yet she might well know more of her husband's dealings and situation than they thought. She also had a right to know that someone was trying to find her husband's murderer and bring him to justice.

There was something melancholy about Daniel Bonneviot's house. Even from the outside, it showed little sign of care, though it was well-built, fronting the street like a prize-fighter staring down an opponent. Inside, all was clean, but somewhat old-fashioned. The home of a bachelor, you might say. A man who had inherited his father's home and furniture and been content to let things be as they always had been. No sign of a woman's touch either. Did Bonneviot ever entertain? Did any save business associates come here at all?

Mrs. Bonneviot received Foxe in the parlour. Though she wore conventional mourning attire, she showed no other sign of sadness or grief. Her voice, as she greeted her visitor, was low and firm. A tallish woman. Neat in her appearance and with a good figure. None would ever call her beautiful, but neither was there anything to justify the epithet of ninny the alderman had bestowed upon her.

They exchanged polite greetings, Foxe added the appropriate words of condolence and she invited him to sit. A maid brought tea.

'You wished to speak with me about my husband, sir?'

'Indeed. The mayor and certain other notable men of the city have asked me to see if I can help bring the murderer of your husband to justice.'

An odd look, almost defiant. She knew what she was about to say would not be either expected or conventional.

'I do not condone murder, sir. Yet whoever did this deed has given me a great benefit, even though he will not know of it. He has given me my freedom at last.'

Here was a surprise indeed.

'Your freedom, madam?'

'My husband was a bully and a tyrant, sir. I know he never loved me, but love and marriage rarely go together outside the pages of books. I do not know whether he even liked me much. He married me for my dowry, as many men do. Sometimes a true regard and affection builds between husband and wife over the years. In our case, it did not.'

'I am sad to hear that. Yet you had children.'

'One child. A son. Eliza is my step-daughter, and she despises me as her father taught her. It would not be seemly for me to talk of matters of the bedchamber. I will say though that my husband always had what he wished and was not unwilling to use force to get it.'

'It was really your family's business I wished to discuss.'

'Then you have wasted your time, sir. I know almost nothing of it. My husband held the opinion that a wife's task was to provide a comfortable home, no more. I often heard him say that the feeble brains of the female sex were unsuitable for matters of importance.'

'You never noticed for yourself what was happening? His warehouse and offices appear to be next door.'

'He kept me a virtual prisoner, as he did his daughter, until she finally married – against his wishes, so that he cut her off from that day. Though he did not want my company, he would not have anyone else have it. I have no friends in this city, sir, and few acquaintances.

Now he is dead, as soon as I may I will leave and return to my family home in Hertfordshire, shaking the dust of this place off the soles of my feet as I leave.'

'And your son …?'

'I do not even know where he is. When he visited us last, my husband ordered him from the house and vowed he should never return. He also cut him out of any inheritance. It did not do to defy my husband's commands. None who did so ever escaped punishment.'

'Might your step-daughter know where he is? Does he even know of his father's murder?'

'My answer is the same to both questions, Mr. Foxe. I do not know. I am sorry to be such an unsatisfactory witness, but you must blame my husband and not me. Though, in truth, if I knew the name of his killer and could tell you exactly where to find him, I am unsure that I would do so.'

'I am truly sorry that you feel thus, madam, though I believe I might have felt the same in similar circumstances. You have been most cruelly mistreated. I cannot put any of that right, nor will I insult you by talking of abstract notions of justice. Yet I feel a great sadness that in our day any husband might treat his wife as yours has dealt with you.'

'You know, Mr. Foxe … I think I even believe you. I am glad you came to see me, for you have restored a little … a very little … of my belief in human kindness. I doubt we will meet again, nor can I wish you success in your investigations, for the reasons I have explained. Yet I wish you well as a person, sir. Do you have a wife?'

'No, madam.'

'Then you should take one, sir. There are few men today worthy of the love of a woman. You should not deprive our sex of even one of them.'

THE FABRIC OF MURDER

Chapter Five

Hidden Knowledge

'TO BE HONEST WITH YOU, Foxe, I'm somewhat disappointed.'

In Foxe's experience, there were two kinds of book collectors. There were those for whom possession was all. Some bought many books, some few, but all were willing to pay almost any amount for something upon which they had set their hearts. Then, having bought it, they retreated into some inner sanctum to gloat over their purchase as a miser contemplates his gold. For the second category, it was finding and securing some addition to their collection which mattered most. These were like hunters, filled with the joy of the chase and maybe even a little sad when the quarry was at length run to earth and secured.

Alderman Halloran was definitely in the first group. His was a working library. Indeed, he seemed often to take far more interest in searching through his books than running his business. Foxe had asked him about this once. He received the enigmatic reply that the success of his business depended in large part on his purchases of books, not the other way around.

'Alderman,' Foxe protested, 'it was but an initial visit. I have had scant time to search. I do not normally make so much as a mention of possible new purchases to anyone, until I arrive at their door with chosen volumes already in my possession. It is only because I know how eager you are for fresh discoveries that I told you at all.'

'I'm sorry, Foxe. I should not have spoken thus. It is good of you to tell me about these things. Of course, if you could but mention the source of these fresh volumes, I might well be able to …'

Foxe laughed. 'You will not catch me that way, Alderman. You know I make it an inflexible rule never to reveal the source of what I buy.'

Alderman Halloran smiled and looked rueful. 'Suppose I should have known. Well, you know I am not interested in old manuscripts, even with fine illuminations. Books on alchemy? No, not for me. I dare say you will find others eager enough for both those categories. I am a Freemason, as you no doubt know, but I do not collect books on the Craft. I can ask in my Lodge and elsewhere to see if others are, if you wish. Natural philosophy. You said there were some on that subject? That is much more to my taste, especially if they bear on the system of understanding pioneered by Sir Isaac Newton.'

'I did.'

'I recall you once asked me why I spent so much on books, both in time and money. It seemed to me then that you expected a merchant and man of business to have quite different interests. That I should be always in my counting-house or warehouse.'

'I was somewhat curious, Alderman. I know you to be a most successful yarn merchant. That did not seem to be consistent with collecting books as you do. Of course, I have some customers who value books for their bindings, the beauty of the pages or their antiquity. They collect books as others collect paintings or statues. Yet, if I am not mistaken, it is the content of a book which interests you.'

'You are not mistaken, Foxe. Our times are marked by constant and rapid change, and not just in knowledge of the natural world and its principles. Men who can make use of such knowledge in practical ways often become rich and successful. They invent new means of manufacture, transport and use of all the other raw materials of this country's wealth. I am ever interested in how I might improve my own business thus. If I do not do it and others do, they will gain an advantage I might well be unable to match. In time, Foxe, much of the labour of men will be replaced by machines able to work faster and without ceasing for rest. We are already seeing such machinery in use in the worsted trade elsewhere. If Norwich lags behind, it will lose its pre-eminence.'

'I will make a list of such books and bring it to you when I can, Alderman. I seem to recall there were more than a few. The owner is not selling his whole library, as I think I mentioned. He has a pressing need for some extra funds at present. I have promised to find the money for him with the loss of as few volumes as possible.'

'Gambling debts, I'll warrant. Or some demanding mistress. Hold on! I believe I heard that Lord and Lady Tomitt have the most grandiose plans for rebuilding Tomitt Towers in the Gothick fashion. They must need a good deal of money for that. Tomitt's father was Grand Master of the Thetford Lodge as well.'

'Those who fish often do so in vain, Alderman, as I am sure you know.'

'Oh, very well, Foxe. Bring me what you think I might like and I will probably be persuaded, as so often with you. But find something more exciting, and you will find me more eager.'

'There is one thing, Alderman. A puzzle.'

'You and your puzzles, Foxe! Whatever now.'

'Have you ever come across a bay of shelving made to conceal something behind it? Made unusually shallow, for example.'

The alderman looked at Foxe in an odd way. Then, having made up his mind, he walked towards the far corner of his library, beckoning Foxe to follow.

'Many of us indulge in … how may I put it? … Books on subjects we would not wish to be on show for a casual visitor to stumble across. And before you get the wrong notion, let me make it clear I do not speak of erotica. I imagine every gentleman has a few volumes of that sort – even you, I dare say. No, what I am speaking of are the kind of books whose possession might arouse unwanted speculation. A sober clergyman might have a secret interest in the occult, for example. He would not wish his parishioners, let alone his bishop, to suspect as much.'

'And your secret interest, Alderman? Not magick, surely!'

'Of course not! Still, I have a position to maintain. It would hurt my business if people thought I held unusual or, especially, heretical religious views. I am trusting you here, Foxe. You are aware of that?'

'Indeed, Alderman, and I am flattered. Have no fear. My own private views on many topics, secular and spiritual, would not bear close scrutiny by those of an orthodox disposition.'

They had come to a set of shelves set into a narrow space between a window and the end wall of the room. There was nothing odd about them, so far as Foxe could see, until … ah, there was that same odd regularity in the size and layout of these volumes. Alderman Halloran leaned forward slightly. He counted six books from the left of the third shelf from the floor, then placed two fingers on the top of the book thus selected.

'Observe,' he said. When he pulled his fingers forward, there was a faint click. The book itself seemed to pivot forwards and the right edge of this whole set of shelves swung an inch or so away from its normal place. Then, reaching into the space, the alderman pressed some other release. Thus he could swing the shelves outwards to reveal a duplicate set of shelving behind. The books on these hidden shelves were as irregular in size and binding as you would expect. Nor were all the shelves full. This private section still had space for a good few additions.

'Some years ago, Foxe, I met a most learned man. He was a refugee from persecution in his native land come to our shores to find liberty of conscience. He it was who first stimulated my interest in the ideas of those whose reasoning was not limited by the claims of churches or religious authority. Like his friends, he relied only on reason to be his guide in all matters, especially in understanding the laws of the natural world. I was entranced. Yet he gave me the most solemn advice never to reveal my thoughts to any but a chosen few. He had been chased half across Europe and must live the life of a fugitive even here.'

'It was sound advice.'

'It was. Even in the time of the great Sir Isaac Newton, many claimed the revelations of the bible contained all knowledge needed. The churches feared for their authority. Their influence would be undermined if statements based on supposed divine revelation proved to be untrue. It is not always easy to disentangle discoveries in natural philosophy from theological dispute.'

'The churches saw men of reason and science as heretics or atheists?'

'Yes. Perhaps some scholars or wealthy gentlemen can afford to ignore disapproval. They do not face the threat of customers going elsewhere. I have learned to appear the most typical of merchants on the outside. I do not deny my true interests. I make sure never to be where I must reveal them. Men say I am a presbyterian in religion. That sect does not demand any set profession of faith. Thus I may attend their services, without making myself a hypocrite in my own eyes.'

'I thank you again, Alderman. I will not betray you. And now that you have shown me this trick, I may have more to report on my next visit.'

'Beware of over-confidence! The carpenter who made this for me said he had made several such devices. Yet he always took care that each should have a release mechanism that was unique. You must not assume the shelves in the library you are dealing with are released in exactly the same manner. There is still a puzzle for you to solve.'

#

On his way home, Foxe considered his next moves. He would return to the earl's library as soon as he could, of course, but first he needed to make better progress in the investigation of Bonneviot's. Too much was still unexplained. The man had been hard on many people, but that had always been his way. Why should anyone decide to kill him now? If any had hated him so much, they must have had opportunity to do him harm long ago. In the end, Foxe decided his next step should be to visit Eliza Swan. It was long odds, but she could not be ignored. He could see no reason why she might have suddenly wished her father dead, though she had probably done so many times over the years. Still, she might at least know something of the tensions within his household. Bonneviot had treated both wife and daughter as chattels. He had been ready to strike his wife if she went against his wishes – perhaps he used his daughter in a similar way. He had even thrown his only son out of the house and his inheritance, when it was clear he would not bow to his father's demands. No, he was even more the domestic dictator than his father had been. Was that alone enough to lead to his death?

Foxe made a detour to call again at Kitty Catt's house. Since it was still some time before the hour of dinner, he was fortunate to find her at home. Yet there she was, wearing a neat day-gown of flowered worsted and looking for all the world like the daughter of a prosperous merchant, since that, indeed, was what she was. Her parents, now both dead, had left their two daughters very well provided. At the moment, she was looking over her lines for her next performance.

'It's no use expecting to be invited to dine with me, Ash,' she began at once. 'This evening I dine at Lady Wakeham's home. But since I have no performance tonight, and she has the habit of dining late, that leaves me …' She looked at the small clock on the mantle in the room. '… quite two hours of freedom.'

Foxe would have assured her that he had not come seeking an invitation to dinner, but she went on before he could speak.

'I received your letter, dear Ash, and am, as they say, quite at your disposal. My sister was green with envy that you asked to take me to the ball.' Yes, she would not have been able to resist imparting that news on the instant. 'You had better have a similar gift for her when you see her next. Indeed, if she did not so much enjoy a certain other kind of encounter with you …' Here she looked at the front of Foxe's breeches. '… I declare she would be quite unwilling to forgive you for giving me the invitation first.'

Foxe shook his head. 'I suppose it never occurred to you to remain silent on the matter for a day or so.'

'Not for an instant!'

'I suppose I ought to have known. But I have come here indeed upon that matter, Kitty. Will you be free one day soon to accompany me to a certain mercer's shop? I thought we might go as an indulgent husband buying a small – yes, small, Kitty. Heed the word – gift for his young wife.'

'Which shop?' Kitty was all business in a moment.

'I am told it was once owned by a Mr. Swan and is now run by his widow.'

Kitty clapped her hands together in delight.

'That is quite the best and most fashionable mercer's shop in the city! How kind of you to take me there to purchase material for the new gown I will need to accompany you to the ball. It must needs be something unusual, even striking. Rich, naturally, but all the other ladies will have gowns of rich silk and the like. No, this gown must stand out.'

Damnation! He should have thought of that. He could only hope the visit would be worth what it would undoubtedly cost him.

'It is also quite the best place to buy the present you owe my sister too.'

Worse and worse!

'She has jewels a-plenty, but cloth for a new gown – or even two – might just soften her mood towards you somewhat.'

'Kitty! I am not made of money. I will buy you sufficient for a ball gown. I will even buy material to dress your sister – though she must have more gowns already than she can ever wear. But I will not be milked like some placid goat. Even I have my limits as far as the Catt sisters are concerned. Drive too hard a bargain and it may be the last we make.'

Kitty looked at him steadily for a moment. 'Very well,' she said, 'but you should know both of us well enough by now to understand that, while we may tease, we love you too well to inflict any real harm.'

'Thank you, my dear. Now, I should leave you to make ready for your engagement. Shall I call for you at eleven? It will be best if you dress as the young wife of a wealthy merchant, for we want Mrs. Swan to deal with us herself.'

'Eleven it is. But you do not escape so easily, Ash. I told you I have quite two hours free before I need to dress for dinner. More than enough time to enjoy your most … outstanding … talents.' She had leaned forward swiftly and seized him in a way that he could not escape without the risk of great pain. Now her fingers were making her intentions still more obvious. Foxe surrendered.

When Foxe finally left her house, nearly two hours later, Kitty was still curled up contently in the nest they had made amongst the bedclothes. For once, she seemed well satisfied with his efforts. And that was good, for he was unsure he could have managed another bout right away.

Foxe had intended to visit Gracie the next afternoon. It was now obvious that he should postpone that. If Kitty sent word to her sister about the way she had spent this afternoon – as she certainly would – he doubted he would escape Gracie's demands for equal treatment. He needed a goodly period of time to regain his strength.

Chapter Six

Into the Past

The Misses Calderwood had known Foxe since his childhood, and would, as always, be delighted by a visit. He knew that, like many elderly people, they slept little and rose early. Nevertheless, he delayed his visit to them until the most polite time of day. These ladies might be old, and they had never been wealthy, but they deserved as much consideration as any others.

Thus it was that Foxe rose at the usual hour the next day and dressed as elegantly as ever. The ladies still appreciated a well-dressed gentleman with shapely calves. Then he took his normal route to The Swan, coffee and the newspaper. Today, his stay was but an hour before he set off again towards the city's brooding, Norman castle and the streets between there and the cathedral. The way down to the river was steepest here, but that had not deterred people from building some fine houses along the way. In back lanes and alleys more modest houses survived, crammed into spaces left by the grand dwellings. They crept between the mansions and gardens of the gentry and the clergy who served the cathedral.

It was to one of these that Foxe made his way. Once it must have been a small timbered cottage of the type to be found throughout Norfolk. Now, alas, the thatched roof was dark with moss and damp. The great beams had also lost much of the pitch that had kept out the weather, and the wattled walls stood in sore need of a fresh coat of lime wash.

Foxe banged hard on the door, though he feared it might not withstand such an assault. Both ladies were somewhat hard of hearing. What income they lived on he could not imagine, for their school had closed down more than a decade ago. Perhaps one of the city's charities provided for them. If he could find out which, he might discreetly add something of his own.

A skinny girl wearing a cut-down dress and an apron that had seen better years, not just days, opened the door then stood silent, as if she could not quite recall what came next. Foxe gave his name. He waited. She waited. At last he asked if he might be allowed to enter and speak with the ladies of the house. The maid considered this for a moment, then stood back and let him pass inside. Then, still in complete silence, she pointed to a room to his left and disappeared further within. In a moment, she was back.

'They says you must follow me to where they are, sir. They also wants me to tell you they be right glad you've come. Few enough comes to visit them now – and never such gentleman as yourself while I've bin 'ere. Then I'm to bring tea, they says, though where I'm to find that I 'as no notion.'

'Here,' Foxe said, giving her five whole shillings. 'Go to the shops in Tombland. Whatever money is left, you may keep for your trouble.'

The girl's eyes rounded like saucers and she rushed away, afraid he might change his mind.

The Misses Calderwood were just as he recalled them. Older and more shrunken now, but still as alert and excited as they were whenever he managed to visit them. Hannah, the elder by two years, wore an old-fashioned mobcap and huddled in a shawl. Her sister Abigail scorned more than a scrap of lace over her hair, white now where once it had been auburn, and peered at him through a pair of spectacles perished askew on her nose.

'Ladies,' Foxe said. 'I thank you for your condescension and willingness to forgive me coming unannounced.'

'He always did have pretty manners,' Miss Abigail said to her sister, speaking as if Foxe was not there. 'Dresses well too.' She turned to Foxe. 'Well, sit you down Ashmole. Stop looming over us like some great lummox.'

'Of course,' Miss Hannah replied, 'None of that counted for much. He might look as if butter wouldn't melt in his mouth, but he was still a naughty child. Sneaky too. He'd look you in the eye and tell you lies enough to make Satan blush.'

The two old women regarded their visitor in a way that indicated he might be older, even richer, but they doubted that his morals had improved.

'So, what do you want, young Ashmole?' It was Hannah again. 'You never did anything without a reason, even if no one else could see what it might be.'

'Especially then,' Abigail said. 'His mind was like a corkscrew for directness. I never knew a more devious child.'

'Mind you, Abby, the boy wasn't wicked or malicious. Artful, I grant you. Devious like you said. Naughty too – though I never trusted any boy who wasn't – but not bad inside. He might never take the highway when he could slip along the lanes unnoticed, but he usually tried to reach some good end.'

'Remember that time we found him bringing a salve to cure Meggy Wimpole's boils and putting it on her himself? It would have been a kind act, if he hadn't persuaded her to take her dress and shift off to make the job easier.'

'Still, I was sad to see him go to a proper school after his uncle died.'

'Changed his life, that did. Where did that uncle get all his money, d'you reckon?'

'No idea. Probably something shady.'

All this Foxe endured with a good grace. He knew they were teasing him, even though all they said was true enough. He had always found cunning superior to fighting as a way to get what you wanted. And though Meggy Wimpole was grubby, none too bright and her boils disgusting, she was unusually well-developed for her age. It was too good a chance to pass over.

By this time, a clattering in the next room suggested the skinny maid had returned and was doing her best to get a kettle to boil for tea. Since that might take some time, Foxe decided he should start before it arrived.

'Master Bonneviot,' Foxe said. 'Do you remember him?' There was no point in pretending any other reason for his visit. They were far too sharp for that. To dissemble would be to insult their minds.

'Father or son,' Miss Hannah said at once. 'Both were master weavers, you know.'

'Let's start with the father.'

The two ladies looked at one another.

'How would you describe him, Hannah?'

'You start, Abigail.' It was clear neither found the topic easy.

'Well ... Jerome Bonneviot was a grown man by the time we knew him, Ashmole. Already a master weaver and quite a successful one. His family had been weavers before him and he'd served his apprenticeship with an uncle somewhere. But he was never an easy man, being a strict Calvinist or something like.'

'Not only that,' Miss Hannah added. 'His life hadn't been easy, I understand. Daniel was the only child of his marriage to survive to adulthood. By then, old Jerome was an embittered man. His wife had died in her last child-bearing and he was alone, but for the boy. They say he became obsessed with religion towards the end. We're not so sure, are we Abby?'

'Odd kind of religion, if you asks me. Jerome Bonneviot gave his son a fine start in the weaving trade, no doubt about that. Then, for some reason, he refused to do more. Once the boy's apprenticeship was over, he made the lad fend for himself. Old Jerome's money was all left to charities, not his family.'

'Daniel, his son, grew up showing most of the worst aspects of his father's character and few of the better ones,' Miss Hannah went on. 'His first wife gave him a daughter, but all the other children she bore soon died. Then she followed them. I call that a merciful release. Daniel was never kind to any woman, as I heard tell. Still, he was quick to marry again and marry well – at least in terms of money. His new wife soon bore him the son he craved. After that, he lost interest in both of them. Young George's mother suffered poor health for a long time after he was born, so the boy was mostly raised by his older step-sister. Even later, his mother still struggled and needed the step-daughter to help.'

'That was what Daniel said. Whether it was true was another matter.' It was Abigail again. 'His daughter was like his wife: his property and don't anyone forget it. She was maybe ten years old when George was born. The old man forced her to stay at home until the lad could begin his apprenticeship. About twelve he was then, so she would be in her early twenties. She never did have many suitors. Her father drove them away. Nor was she beautiful enough or rich enough for any of them to want to defy him. The minute young Daniel left home, she went too. Married the first man she could find, though he was perhaps twenty years older than her.'

'It wasn't a bad move though, Abigail. Her husband was a good man and they had two – or was it three? – children who survived childhood. When he died, she kept the business on as well.'

'What business was that?' Foxe enquired. He knew the answer already, of course, but it was sometimes best to pretend ignorance. If you said you knew the answer, people added nothing. If you pretended ignorance, they might tell you many things to augment your knowledge.

'Samuel Swan was a mercer and haberdasher, with a shop on Pottergate. His widow keeps it now. That's Eliza Bonneviot, as was, Daniel Bonneviot's step-daughter. A good shop, but far above our means. Eliza Swan knows her cloth.' Foxe made a mental note to warn Kitty of this fact. For the moment, he wanted to hear more about Daniel Bonneviot's household.

'So Daniel went as an apprentice at twelve or so,' he said.

'That's right,' Miss Hannah said. 'He'd come to us before then. His father could have afforded better, of course, but, as dissenters, his family were barred from the professions and the universities. That is why so many became prominent in business. The father had us teach Daniel his letters, reading and writing enough for business and simple arithmetic for casting accounts. After that, off he went to London.'

'London!' Foxe was surprised.

'We told you the Bonneviots were Huguenots, didn't we?' Abigail said. 'Lots of them in London, I heard. Anyway, old Mr. Bonneviot had relatives in London ...'

'In Smithfield.' Her sister always liked to be precise.

'Yes, my dear. In Smithfield. A master weaver of great renown. It cost a pretty penny to apprentice the boy to such a master, so we heard, even if he was kin. Still, he taught the lad well. Daniel Bonneviot became a fine craftsman in the weaving way.'

'What was Daniel like as a boy?' Foxe asked.

'Difficult,' Miss Hannah said. 'Stubborn, cruel and willful. Always fighting with the other boys. If you said or did anything Daniel took amiss, his answer was ever to use his fists. No one wronged him and escaped revenge. There was a great stock of anger inside the boy. Yet he was clever enough and learned well.'

'Not a likeable boy,' her sister added. 'His father could seem grim and withdrawn, but usually treated others fairly enough. The son was scornful and arrogant. He cared nothing for anyone else, so long as he got what he wanted.'

'So he did his apprenticeship and came back to his father as a journeyman.' Foxe needed to move the conversation along.

'Oh no, Ashmole,' Miss Abigail said. 'I think he was a journeyman in London … or was it Halifax?'

At this point, the maid came in. It seemed she had at last obtained boiling water enough to bring in dishes – none too clean – and a rather old-fashioned teapot. She placed all on the table and added a dish containing some tea leaves.

'Tea?' Miss Hannah said. 'Where on earth did you find that? I thought we had used our last tea – when was it? August? September?'

'To my mind, it was August a twelvemonth ago,' Miss Abigail said. 'Where was it, girl? It must be quite old.'

'I sent your maid to buy some,' Foxe said. 'Think of it as a small gift.'

The sisters looked at him in amazement. 'There must be four shillings' worth here,' Miss Hannah said.

'Three shilling an' thruppence,' her maid said. 'Your visitor said as I might keep the rest for going.'

'Indeed I did. Now, which of you ladies will make the tea?'

'I will,' both said together.

Foxe laughed. 'Miss Hannah is the elder, I believe. Perhaps she should do it.'

When they had made the tea, both sipped at it gingerly – though in truth the water had not been quite at the boil and the dishes cooled it quickly.

'Thank you, dear Ashmole,' Miss Abigail said. 'To be honest, I never though to taste good tea again. It's too expensive for us. Are you so rich you can give it away as you have?'

Foxe nodded.

'Shall we ask how he came so rich?' she said to her sister. 'I warrant there was a trick in it somewhere.'

'Drink your tea, dear,' her sister said. 'It would not be polite to question someone who has given us such a gift, even if I do share your doubts about Ashmole's way of life. I hear he consorts with the Catt sisters nowadays. There's a pair of beauties! Gracie runs that terrible house and Kitty shows herself to all on the stage. There isn't a single scruple or any moral sense in either of them … Do they make good lovers, Ashmole?'

It took several minutes of coughing for Foxe to recover from that question, for his tea had near choked him in his surprise. Fortunately, his confusion and discomfort freed him from the need for an immediate reply.

'You were saying Bonneviot … that's Daniel, I mean … served his period as journeyman in London,' he managed at last. 'Did Jerome not want his son to succeed him in his business here?'

For a moment, he feared one or other would press him on the other matter, but it seemed they had tired of the game.

'That was typical of old Mr. Bonneviot,' Miss Hannah said. 'He'd started with naught save his skill, so he determined his son should do the same. Before the boy returned, his father had sold his goods and business and, so the rumour went, devoted himself to study and religion. Maybe the father reckoned he'd discharged his duty to his son by giving him a good apprenticeship. They could never have worked together. Jerome might have been the owner of the business, but Daniel wouldn't suffer anyone to give him orders. Maybe the old man knew what his son was like and wasn't going to subject himself to that sort of treatment in his old age.'

'Never left him more'n a pittance when he died,' Miss Abigail added, 'and he was quite a rich man. All his other wealth went to setting up his various charities. His son Daniel had to make his own way.'

'But he did,' Foxe said.

'Daniel Bonneviot had a ferocious need to win at whatever he did,' Miss Hannah said. 'Same when he was a boy. And if he couldn't win by fair means, he'd still win.'

'Daniel had a son too,' Foxe said.

'Him!' Miss Abigail's scorn was obvious. 'His mother spoiled him, though it cost her a fair few bruises. George must do his apprenticeship in London, same as his father. George must be journeyman elsewhere too. As Daniel decreed, so George must obey. Then only a few weeks ago, his father drove him out of the house without mercy. We heard he gave the boy a hundred pounds and told him he never wanted to see or hear of him again. That money was all he should ever have. I wonder where all his wealth will go now?'

'Do we know he cut the boy off from his inheritance?' Miss Hannah asked her sister. 'All this happened quite soon before Mr. Bonneviot died. Would he have had time to change his will? After all, even when it was clear the lad wouldn't agree to follow his father's bidding in everything, he still seemed to stick by him … for a while.'

'I don't think the boy was ever going to have an inheritance. If you ask me, it was to be as it had been with his father. He must make his own way,' her sister replied. 'Daniel never accepted young George wasn't interested in weaving. Nothing else counted for him. He didn't change his mind for anyone. As I see it, the boy had been given some time to come to his senses and do as he was told. It seems he hadn't. Time was up.'

'And the other thing ...?'

'Well, yes. We all had our doubts about George in that way. Still that's only imagination and gossip, dear. He may yet ask some young lady to marry him.'

Miss Hannah snorted in a very unladylike manner at that. 'Young lad, more likely ...!'

'Where did George go when his father threw him out?' Foxe asked.

'I'm afraid we've no idea, Ashmole. He may have gone to London or somewhere.'

'Were there any other children?'

'Only the step-sister. She may know something, but I doubt it.'

They knew no more. Daniel Bonneviot's wife had, it seemed, made little impression on them or anyone else in Norwich. George, the only son, had been away in London for years, completing his apprenticeship. Miss Abigail eventually added the gossip that he had nurtured hopes of becoming an actor at one time, but the local theatres had all rejected him.

That had been the main difference between father and son, it seemed. The father set his mind on something and drove himself – and everyone else – until he achieved it, whether by fair means or otherwise. His son wished and hoped and dreamed of great things, but showed neither the talent nor the energy to do more.

Had an enraged father thrown that failure in the son's face? Might that have been enough to stir the younger man to take his revenge? He would never have confronted his father openly. Foxe felt sure of that. But an attack from behind in a dark street …? That might be another matter altogether. Even so, Foxe couldn't see this young man they had suggested was limp and effeminate as the murderer. To cut someone's throat, even in the dark, demanded resolution and suddenness. Besides, Bonneviot had been a powerful man and of a good height. He had been taken by surprise, to be sure, but few people have the strength to slit another's throat so quickly there is no chance for them to call out or fight back.

No, from all Foxe had heard, George Bonneviot did not have the makings of a killer, unless it should be by some secret poison. From the description of him given both by the Misses Calderwood and Gracie Catt, Foxe had come to regard him as much too feeble. He could, of course, have paid some ruffian to do it – that was a point worth investigating – but he would not himself be capable of such a deed.

Chapter Seven

The Fruits of Deception

WHEN FOXE ENTERED THE COFFEE HOUSE at ten the next morning, Brock was waiting. Since he had already finished his coffee and discarded the newspaper, it looked as if he had been there for some time.

'Thought you might be in earlier than this.' He sounded irritated. Brock didn't like to be kept waiting.

'Why?' Foxe said. 'This is quite a respectable hour to come here. I also have an appointment at eleven, so that leaves me a reasonable time to drink a dish of coffee and peruse the papers.'

Foxe had not dressed in quite such an elegant manner this morning. He needed to look the kind of customer Mrs. Swan would want to serve in person, but not the kind she would remember for too long afterwards.

'Do you have news?' he asked Brock.

'Wouldn't have come here if I hadn't. Nothing significant from those of Bonneviots' men I've spoken to. They're angry about being owed money and want their due – be sure of that. But that's a simple matter of justice, in their eyes. I can't see them doing more than breaking a few windows to let off steam. Trade seems brisk enough and a good weaver is always in demand. Of course, the ones that remain are the ones 'e treated better. Those 'e already threw out have either left Norwich and gone elsewhere or found a new master. To be honest with you, I don't see any of 'em being angry enough with the man to kill 'im.'

'That bothers me, Brock. If trade is so good, why was Bonneviot laying men off at all? Forget the useless ones. Any master would get rid of them as soon as he could. It's the others I'm thinking of: the ones who soon found a new master.'

'See your drift. If another master was glad to have them at short notice, they must be good – or good enough.'

'Anyone else you talked to?'

'I wanted to talk to his foreman at the warehouse, but he said he was too busy. Now there's another odd thing.' Brock's frown was so ferocious the waiter coming with Foxe's usual coffee stepped back in alarm.

'Ignore my friend,' Foxe said to the lad. 'He suffers from stomach cramps brought on by too much drink.'

'I don't drink much more than you do,' Brock said. 'Besides, this coffee would soon give any man the bellyache.'

'Go on, Brock,' Foxe said. 'You said something about Bonneviot's foreman was odd.'

'Not him so much as his situation. His employer has just been murdered, yet 'e's rushed off 'is feet. Doin' what? I'd also say the man is happy as they come. Now, he may not have liked Bonneviot – 'ated his guts even – but he'd worked for him for more than ten years, as

I heard. Now 'is master's dead and the son doesn't show any interest in the business. You'd expect an old hand like this cove – Jack Astle, he's called – to be worried about 'is job. But 'e isn't, it seems. Already staying on in the same position.'

'Now that is odd, I grant you. Is the widow keeping the business on?'

'That's what I rushed here to tell you, only you were frolicking in bed with one of them Catt sisters, I guess, and not most keen to get up.'

'For your information, Brock – not that it is any business of yours – I slept alone last night and this is always the time I come in here. Go on, my friend, and keep your thoughts to yourself.'

'Keep your wig on. Here's the real news. I've heard from several of the weavers who used to work for Bonneviot that his business, stock and premises have already ended up in the hands of someone else. They're to work on as if nothing had happened, it seems.'

'There wouldn't be time to obtain probate, surely.'

'I wouldn't know about that. All I could find out is that some person is already running the business just as before. I imagine the executors agreed. A going concern is worth a hell of a lot more than one that's already closed down. Or one so beset with uncertainty no one will place orders.'

'True enough, I suppose. I don't imagine you found out who this new owner is going to be?'

'Not for certain. But I did 'ear a certain Mr. Callum Burford mentioned. He's a master weaver, but in a much smaller scale of doing business than Bonneviot was. If 'e's going to be the owner, I'd like to know where he's getting the money from.' Brock paused. 'There's something else strange. I got good contacts amongst the bargees and wherrymen, as you well know, seein' as 'ow I owns a good few of their boats. Most of the cloth from around here goes to London, a good deal of it along the roads. The rest goes by boat to Yarmouth, then by ship into London.'

Foxe interrupted. 'Is there no local trade?'

'Nothing enough to keep all Norwich's folk busy. Now, our trade has been in the hands of the London merchants for a good time. Not that some 'aven't tried to break free, but only a few seem to have managed it and then not for long.'

'So lots of wagons, packhorse trains and the like along the London road and the rest to Yarmouth.'

'Right. But Bonneviot, it seems, was one of those who 'ated the London merchants most. He had to deal with them, but it stuck in 'is throat. Well, for the past few months, 'e's sent almost nothing for London or anywhere else by boat. Can't say about the roads, mind. But it seems peculiar. If it was all going by road, 'e sold so much 'e'd take a good many of the wagons and pack-horses just for 'is own goods, with few left over for the other master weavers. It looks as if 'e was lettin' finished goods pile up in 'is warehouse. Now, what merchant does that unless 'e 'as no other choice?'

'Good work, Brock. Now sit quiet and let me think a while.' Foxe drank some more coffee, then leant back in his chair and closed his eyes. He remained like that, not moving, for a full five minutes at least. All at once he sat up, opened his eyes and turned to Brock in excitement.

'Thanks to you, Brock, I can see I've been on the wrong track. I even suspect I'm wasting my time this morning with Mrs. Swan too. Still, I can't disappoint my friend, so I'll still need to go. I just hope it doesn't cost me as much as I fear it may.'

'Hope you know what you're going on about,' Brock growled. 'Hell's Teeth if I know.'

'Brock. Forget the weavers and the foreman. The answer isn't there. You can forget about the new buyer or owner or whatever as well. I'll find his name from elsewhere. What I want you to do next is vital.'

'What is it then?'

'I need you to find a man who has been willing to kill someone for payment, Brock.'

'Got someone you dislike, have you? Look, Foxe. You could find twenty or more men willing to do that if you paid them enough. Can't you help me narrow it down a bit.'

'Not someone who would kill, Brock, someone who has – and recently. Someone who seems to have more cash about him than he should. If I'm right, it won't be the kind of person you or I would choose – assuming either of us would stoop so low. It has to be someone a stranger could find. Someone desperate and not too expensive. Someone others would give as a name if they didn't want to get involved.'

Brock thought a moment, then smiled. 'McSwiggan. That's your man I reckon.'

'Why him, who ever he is.'

'A nasty, verminous, mean, vicious, loud-mouthed shit is who 'e is. Scotsman, so he says, but I don't believe 'e's ever left Norfolk. He's just the type to talk big and take anyone's money for whatever dirty work they needed done. Coming on a man at night from behind and slitting his throat would be exactly McSwiggan's style.'

'Find him! I don't want you to do more than that for now. Find him, find out what he's been up to the past few days and see if anyone has noticed him getting more drunk than usual or having money to burn.'

'Right you are, though 'e don't move in the kind of areas I'd be happy to go into much. Mind if I use one or two others? Reliable blokes.'

'Not at all, Brock. I don't want you getting hurt. Nor your friends either. If it comes to laying hands on this McSwiggan, we'll leave that to the constables. But there won't be any use in doing that without having enough to hang him first. From all you say, I can't see him confessing or – much more important – telling us who paid him to do it.'

'That's true enough,' Brock said. 'He's been in enough tight places to know every trick there is for getting away. Take care! He's a slippery bastard. Unless you have a case not even an elver could slip out of, 'e'll laugh in your face.'

'Right. To it, Brock! That is, unless you want any more of the delicious coffee they sell here.'

'I'd rather drink water straight from the gutters!'

'Be off then. I have to leave soon to meet my wife.'

'Merciful God! You haven't married one of those Catt women, 'as you? Or even both on 'em?'

'Whatever put that idea into your head, Brock? Mrs. Eleanor Foxworth is young and pretty, I grant you, but she is already married to a most respectable gentleman. They have come to our fair city to visit certain relatives. Knowing its renown for the production of fine worsteds, they have also decided to buy material to make Mrs. Foxworth a new gown. They may also look for a similar amount for Mrs. Foxworth's sister, as a gift.'

Brock threw back his head and roared with laughter, thus causing several of the older customers to wake up and look around in surprise. 'I don't know how you thinks these wheezes up. I won't ask who is to play the part of your wife. It 'as to be Kitty. But you're a braver man than most to take her into a mercers!'

'I agree, Brock. But needs must. I just hope my bravery is not tested further than I fear.'

Mrs. Swan turned out to be a gaunt, grey-haired woman, a little above the average in height, but otherwise unremarkable. Her manner veered between oily, obsequious and patronising. It suggested to Foxe that she would do well in the general run of things to leave the selling of her wares to her assistants.

Kitty Catt, of course, played her part to perfection as the pretty ingenue, married to a doting older husband. She had hidden her hair under a mousy brown wig and dressed in a sober, provincial day-gown and petticoat. It was what anyone might expect of someone wearing her best, yet more at home in a far smaller town than Norwich.

As Mrs. Swan brought out swathe after swathe of rich silks and satins, Kitty exclaimed in excitement at every one. Of course, had Mrs. Swan bothered to take note, she might have realised all was not quite as she imagined. This girl she took as naïve rejected all the outdated and remnant stock she was trying to palm off on her. None quite matched the colours Mrs. Foxworth had in mind. They were likely to resemble materials she knew her friends were using. When the shopkeeper brought out several bolts of embroidered and ornamented silk in peculiar dyes of maroon and purple, Mrs. Foxworth seemed first to look on them with delight. Then she said they were far too expensive and showy for their home town of Cheltenham.

Why she picked on this innocent market-town in Gloucestershire, Foxe had no idea. Yet, it seemed to serve well enough. Mrs. Swan clearly knew nothing of the place. She doubtless assumed it to be the sort of small, rural township common throughout the eastern counties of England.

'Lah, Madam! This is indeed lovely, but it will not do to dress so far above our station, will it, dear Mr. Foxworth? That would only excite comment of an envious nature. Nor would I have you waste our money on such expensive cloth. Our small assemblies and balls attract few of the gentry. Yet those who do condescend to appear would never feel it right for a simple merchant's wife to dress more richly than them.'

'Whatever you say, dearest,' Foxe replied. He was trying to catch the tone of a husband willing to indulge his new wife in almost anything. He too had dressed as simply as he could, while retaining the appearance of a gentleman. His brown coat and matching waistcoat were of excellent worsted brocade, but neither displayed the embroidery in gold or silver thread that he loved so much.

For some time, Kitty engaged in the prettiest dithering about her choice between several fabrics of but modest expense. That left Foxe free to draw Mrs. Swan into conversation.

'You show an excellent and extensive knowledge of the fabrics of these parts, madam. I am glad we were recommended by our hosts to come here to make our purchases.'

'You are most kind, Mr. Foxworth. I own that few mercers and haberdashers can match my experience or understanding. My late father and grandfather, you see, were both noted master weavers of this city. I grew up amongst looms and bales of cloth of all kinds.'

'Indeed? A most helpful start for a mercer. I am told that you are, alas, a widow. But perhaps you have a young son you are grooming to succeed you?'

'No, I fear not, sir. My husband and I were blessed with two sons, but both died while still infants. Now only my daughter remains. I am delighted to say, she is now married with children of her own. I will be the last of our line to work in the textile trade.'

'Ah, that is sad. Of course, you mentioned your late father but a moment ago. But perhaps he had a son to succeed him?'

Mrs. Swan's face darkened somewhat, before resuming its professional blandness.

'My mother died when I was young and my father married again. As you can imagine, he was eager to have sons to succeed him. Yet the one who did come – aye, and near cost his mother her life in doing so – has interest neither in business nor cloth.'

Foxe judged it best not to pursue that point further. It would not do to raise Mrs. Swan's suspicions by showing too close an interest in her family.

'So his widow, your step-mother, now runs the family business?'

'Her! She has not the wit of a chicken. No, my father died but a few days ago, sir, and I fear his business is to be sold.'

'Ah, that is sad,' Foxe said. 'Forgive me, madam, for treading on such recent grief in my ignorance. It was but idle conversation. I had no idea I might stray into what cannot fail to be the most painful recollections for you.'

Kitty, despite her quiet murmuring and fluttering over the bolts of cloth, had kept her ears alert. Now she came to Foxe's rescue.

'My dearest husband,' she said. 'I am most grateful for your patience. This is such a large expense that I determined to make the best choice possible. Now, if it is not too much of a strain on your purse …' Here she added a simpering laugh. '… I have chosen a fabric for the gown and two others for the petticoat to go with it. I believe that five or six yards of each one should be ample for my dressmaker to work with.'

What she had chosen was most cleverly done. They bought a simple linen cloth for the lining of the gown and some stiff silk moiré taffeta in a deep tawny colour for the gown itself. For decoration, Kitty chose several yards of rich lace and some matching ribbon. All appeared quite suitable for a wealthy merchant's wife. Even somewhat plain for her apparent hair colour and complexion. Yet Foxe knew that, set off by deep cuffs of the ivory silk and the tumbling mass of auburn curls that were Kitty's trademark, it would look stunning.

Mrs. Foxworth scorned a matching petticoat. Instead, she gave her husband a tiny kiss on the cheek and begged for his forgiveness in selecting a fine silk brocade. This would match the lace and was embroidered with bouquets of yellow roses and swathes of ribbon, picked out with gold wire. To that she added a good, flowered calamanco worsted for the lining.

'Now for my sister's gift,' Mrs. Foxworth said. Her supposed husband winced inwardly, but managed to keep his composure. 'I believe she will look well indeed in this deep maroon silk brocade for the dress. The one with the pattern of bows and ribbons in silver thread. Linen again for the lining, of course.'

Foxe thought of Gracie's mass of dark hair. Her sister had chosen well.

'Perhaps the petticoat might look best in silk brocade also. I think this deep pink would suit. It has a lovely pattern of embroidered flower-sprays. Yes, that will be best. We might take her some striped camblet for lining, I think. Will that not cost too much, Mr. Foxworth?'

Foxe knew he was being let off lightly, so hastened to agree at once that it was within his means. He was deeply suspicious of this meek, restrained version of Kitty, so prudent in spending his money.

An assistant measured out the cloth and Mrs. Foxworth wandered about the shop, still exclaiming over ribbons and buttons of all kinds. Meanwhile Foxe took a last opportunity to pry a little further into Mrs. Swan's affairs.

'It is sad your brother will not follow his father into the same trade, Mrs. Swan …'

'Step-brother,' Mrs Swan interrupted.

'Ah, yes. Step-brother.'

'Since his mother was so often in poor health, my father set me to raise him. It was not what I would have chosen, but I did my best.' Mrs. Swan was clearly rehearsing an old grievance. 'My father gave him a good apprenticeship too. Now his mind is full of nonsense about going on the stage. Is acting a respectable mode of life, Mr. Foxworth?' Foxe agreed that it definitely was not.

'He has turned his back on weaving altogether, so it seems. Not that it would have mattered, in the event.' Mrs. Swan seemed glad of a chance to unburden herself of her feelings. Foxe had noticed before that people spoke of things to a stranger that they would never dream of mentioning amongst their own. They assumed they would never see their hearer again, and he or she would know no one of note to whom they could spread gossip.

'My father was a fine weaver, sir, but a poor man of business. Rash and headstrong in all things, as well I know. Prone to quarrel as well, I am afraid to say. I did what I could, but he would never listen to a woman, be she wife or daughter. Before he died, I understand he had sunk so deep into debt that his business would have been forfeit to his creditors before long. Wife, son, relatives will find little in what remains.'

This was such a sudden and complete revelation that Foxe thought he should change the topic at once. He doubted she would give him the names of those to whom her father owed so much. And to ask would be quite foreign to the character he was playing.

'I believe my wife is ready …'

Mrs. Swan, however, was not so eager to find another topic. 'Of course, due to his quarrel he had to raise more capital. To go into debt is to set yourself at hazard, I say. Still, one was ready to lend him what he needed, as a certain person told me. Now the business is foundered and others must meet the costs.'

'Mrs. Swan. I do beg your pardon, but my wife has been waiting for me some little time, I believe …'

At that, Mrs. Swan seemed to pull herself back to the present, though with some effort. She reckoned up the cost, smiling to herself while she did it. Foxe handed over a pile of gold sovereigns that might have kept a family of poor weavers in a fair way of life for many years. Then, giving strict instructions their purchases were to be delivered to their coachman, who would call the next morning, the couple left.

Neither commented on their thoughts until they were back in Kitty's neat house and awaiting her maid, who was bringing tea.

'Well,' Kitty said. 'Did you like my performance?'

'Perfect as always, my dear. Yet …' But Kitty had broken into peals of laughter.

'Could you but see your face, Ash! I do declare that I have discomforted you as your attentive young wife. Yet she was so careful of your fortune and so modest in her choosing.'

'That's what bothers me, Kitty. I can't help feeling that I am soon to be presented with one more account to settle this day. One that may make the large amount I have already paid seem small in comparison.'

'Large amount? What large amount?'

'Perhaps not large by your normal standards, Kitty dear, but still enough to lighten my pocket a good deal.'

'Did you not like what I bought?'

'In truth, you chose in excellent taste. I am sure you will look ravishing in the dress that you will have made for you. Your sister will also stun any audience in the cloth you chose for her. But …'

'So you would not be ashamed to be seen with either of us at this ball?'

'In no way! I should be honoured to have either you or your sister on my arm, for you would both far outshine the other ladies present.'

'That is good, Ash. And if having one Catt sister on your arm would be such a distinction, to have one on either side must be doubly so. Do you not agree?'

'What! Take both of you!'

'Of course, Ash dear. No woman could possible receive a gift of such magnificence as the fabrics and trims you bought today and not desire the earliest opportunity to show herself off in them.'

Foxe groaned and hid his head in his hands. If he had feared she was up to something, this was far beyond his worst expectations.

'Ash! I will be quite put out if you take on so. You yourself said taking me would be an honour. How can two honours become a disaster?'

'My dear Kitty. I already have something of a doubtful reputation with some persons of note in this city. Not that I have ever sought to make any secret of my relations with you or your sister. Indeed, I have counted your company as something to be shown to all. But to arrive at a ball with the two of you …'

'It is settled, Ash. Gracie and I talked of it yesterday evening and we are sure your reputation, such as it is, will survive. Besides, do you not always make sure each sister receives the same attentions as the other? Speaking of which, my sister not only has news for you, but, hearing of the agreeable time we spent together recently …'

'Kitty! Kitty! I yield. Only let me go now to rest and renew my strength for what your sister has in mind.'

'You make her sound like a wrestler with whom you must contend at peril of your life.'

'That is an excellent analogy! A bout with either of you is enough to test the strength and skill of any man, though the contest is, I own, most sweet. Nay, do not frown, Kitty. For if you may jest with me and tease, may I not do the same with you? Though I dare say I will scandalise the whole of Norwich, I will take both you and your sister to the ball and hold my head high. The ladies will tut and frown, but I vow every man in the place will be consumed with envy. And I will also visit your sister in the next day or so, as I had already determined to do.

When, as I am sure she will, she comes to you to make comparison, I will do my best not to be found wanting.'

'As if we would compare!'

'As if you would not. No, no, Kitty. Delay me no more. For I have much to think about and have neither the time nor the capacity for more distractions.'

And with that, Foxe hurried to the door and out of the house, lest his resolution crumble to nothing at the touch of Kitty's soft fingers.

Chapter Eight

Secret Shelves

FOXE WAITED UNTIL THE EARL'S FOOTMAN HAD WITHDRAWN from the library at Pentelow Hall. Then he crossed the huge room to stand again before the bay of shelving that had attracted his attention on his last visit. He considered that a bad flaw in the design. Had the exterior presented a more uneven appearance, he would never have noticed anything amiss. Still, the sixth and seventh earls probably expected few but invited guests to enter this room. The purpose of the deception had likely been more to deter servants or more curious guests from seeing whatever the shelves concealed. He hoped it would not be lewd books. That would be boring.

Whatever was there, he must first find the release mechanism. It proved no easy matter. As if to make up for allowing the presence of something unusual to be visible, the carpenter had employed great ingenuity in hiding the release. It took Foxe near thirty minutes of pushing, pulling and pressing various books to decide that approach was not going to work. At last he did what he should have done at the start. He stood back, stared at the shelves and considered what he might do in the same situation.

The release must be in a position that would be convenient for use. That ruled out those shelves too high to reach without a ladder, or too low to be seen without bending. None of the wooden framing showed any marks that might indicate a place to press or pull. What was left? The books, of course, but he had tried all of those.

But had he? He had followed the pattern of the alderman's library shelving, despite Halloran's warning. He should have known that the carpenter never used the same method of concealment twice. He had pivoted books forward and backward. He had tried pushing on their spines or feeling along the tops for some hidden lever. What he had not done was take any out of their places altogether.

That was it, of course. On removing the fifth or sixth book from the middle shelf, he felt the wood beneath where it stood and touched metal, not wood. His finger hooked neatly into a gap that allowed part of the metal to be raised like a lever. There was a satisfying click and the right-hand edge of the bay of shelving swung outwards by a space of maybe two inches. Just enough to slide his hand behind.

Another minute or so of feeling around the gap located another metal lever. When he pulled that forward, the whole bay of shelving could be swung outwards like a door. Behind was a space deep enough to contain shelves of a normal size.

To Foxe's relief, the bulk of the hidden books were not erotica. The few that were lay on the topmost shelves. All the rest were unfamiliar to him. Some were in English, some in French, one or two in Latin. None, to his disappointment, had dates within that were more than a hundred years ago. Many had been printed in places like Amsterdam, Leiden or Geneva within the past fifty years or less. They seemed to be books of philosophy, which puzzled him. Why hide philosophical books? Then he stumbled on one book in plain binding with no title. When he opened it, all became plain.

What he had found was a work called 'The Treatise of the Three Imposters'. It was said to be written by an Irishman called John Toland, though that was not established. Foxe had never had a copy in his hands before, but he knew it was a book valued highly by freethinkers. More conventional persons judged it a repository of the rankest blasphemy.

Maybe the rest were books of radical, even revolutionary, ideas. That would be reason enough to hide them. Well, Alderman Halloran had indicated an interest in the works of freethinkers. Foxe would make a list of some of the authors and titles and take it to show him. If these were books of such a nature, he would be the most likely purchaser, since Foxe knew no one else with similar tastes.

He closed up the shelves again. Then he applied himself to finding another dozen or so volumes that he knew he could sell swiftly and for a good price. Those he placed on the central table with the same care as before. He estimated he had now taken books that might fetch some four hundred pounds. That was enough to cover the amount of the draft he had given to the earl. It did not quite match his usual margin of profit, but Foxe was not a greedy man. He could find the five hundred pounds the earl needed and still provide himself with a satisfactory return.

He had finished his selection of books for that day and was about to call for the footman, when he noticed something else odd. On the shelving devoted to books on alchemy, the books stood in the normal order of size. The smallest were on the topmost shelves, the largest at the bottom. Yet at the far edge of the top shelf, two slim volumes were far taller than all the books around them. Indeed, they were so tall that Foxe, standing uncertainly on a library ladder, had the greatest difficulty in extracting them. The only way he could do it was to remove several other volumes first, then tilt each larger book sideways until it was almost flat. They must have been inserted that way, on their sides, then turned upright. That meant several inches of them were hidden behind a band of wooden decoration that fitted between the upper edge of the bookshelf and the ceiling.

Why put these two books onto the shelves in such a way that they could not be removed without the greatest difficulty? The lettering on the spines indicated nothing unusual. Two volumes of yet another set of obscure works on alchemy. Not even a respectable area of enquiry. Foxe thought it was little more than wishful thinking and a desire to claim knowledge that others could not contest.

When he began to leaf through the first volume, he had another surprise. He was used to the habit of some men to add notes of their own to the books they read. Usually, this reduced their value at once. Only in a few cases, where the person making the annotations was famous, was the value of a book increased. Yet what he could see before him was not the normal type of annotation. Most of the pages were free of any kind of note. But where there was a large empty space, or the binder left a blank page to make sure the next chapter opened on a right-hand page, there was writing enough. What these notes might be was obscure. They looked like the receipts used by those wishing to cook a special dish. Or maybe the reminders used by apothecaries in making medicines. Each began with a list of ingredients, then instructions on how to prepare them. That was followed by the right time for steeping the mixture and the amount of boiling water and cold water to use.

It was not foodstuffs. That was clear soon enough. No one adds urine or flowers of sulphur to something to be eaten. Some of the ingredients were also minerals, by the look of them. Others had odd names that meant nothing to Foxe.

Could they be the secret formulae of some alchemist? If that was the case, it might account for any special interest in these volumes. Foxe could find no name or identification of a past owner. Nothing to say whether the person who wrote down these formulae, if that was what they were, was famous or not.

For a while, Foxe continued to leaf through the pages, musing on possible solutions to the mystery. Then, almost on a whim, he put one of the books in the pocket of his coat. He would take it home to examine. He might also show it to one or two people whom he knew had some interest in chemical experiments. They might be able to tell him enough to set a value on these mysterious books and their annotations.

He checked the books on the central table – another dozen – and called the footman. 'Have these volumes packed and delivered as before, if you would be so good. I have also selected one small book to take with me now. It is not easy to identify and value, so I will take it to my shop and allow myself time to consider it in greater depth. Please tell His Lordship that I will reckon up all. Then I will send him another banker's draft to cover what amount goes beyond the last one I left with him.'

'Very good, sir. May I enquire whether the first box of books was packed to your satisfaction?'

'Certainly. All arrived quite undamaged.'

'Then I will see these are packed in the same way. Please remain at your leisure here while I call the earl's carriage to take you home again.'

On his way back into Norwich, Foxe took the mystery book from his pocket. It had been printed and published in Geneva in 1666. He would wager also that some at least of the writing dated from close to that time. There was something old-fashioned about the means of forming the letters and the ink was much faded. That would make what was written here over a hundred years old. And, while the text of the book itself was in French, the notes were in several languages. Sometimes French, sometimes what he thought must be Flemish and once or twice in English. If he was right, these notes had been begun about a hundred years ago in France, then continued in Flemish and English, probably at various times between then and now. The few English notations showed up by their blacker ink and more modern form of handwriting.

The picture he was building was of a secret notebook, used and added to over more than one generation. It was, he thought, written in blank spaces in printed books as another means of keeping its contents hidden. They must have been quite valuable to the ones who wrote them. Even so, they might have no value today. Few in this modern world held alchemy to be more than a primitive form of the chemical science. A sad mixture of genuine experiment with wild phantasies and dreams of infinite power and immortality.

Foxe cursed himself under his breath. The earl had promised to look out the records of book purchases that his father and grandfather had kept. Foxe had forgotten to ask the footman whether this had been done. If he could discover who had sold them these two strange books and when, it might go a long way to help understand such value as they might have.

Almost on a whim, Foxe rapped on the roof of the carriage with his stick to signal a halt. Then he asked the driver to detour so that he could call at the alderman's house. He would leave this annoying book there for his patron to see. He might know what, if anything, these annotations could mean.

Chapter Nine

Losing Heart

THE NEXT MORNING, AT ABOUT ELEVEN, Foxe stepped into the building that housed the presses and offices of The Norfolk Intelligencer. At once he felt himself taken back to the sights and smells of his childhood. His father had been a printer and bookseller. Young Ashmole spent many an hour amongst paper, presses and inks. There he learned the intricacies and secrets of the printer's trade. That should still have been his trade today, had not a near-forgotten uncle made a vast fortune in the sugar plantations of the West Indies. When the uncle died childless, he left all to his nearest male relative, who happened to be his nephew Ashmole.

The young Foxe had no wish to live in such a colonial outpost. Nor did he relish the idea of being the owner of hundreds of slaves – especially if he was not on hand to see how his overseers might treat them. First he sold the plantations and the rum distillery. Then he determined never to put his money where he could not keep a close eye on how it was used in the world.

To become a gentleman with a grand mansion, sweeping parkland and thousand of acres of land under tenancies did not entice the young Foxe either. By this time, in his chosen profession of bookseller, he had known too many such men. Hunting, gambling and racing horses bored him. Being a magistrate and local dignitary repelled him. The very notion of being a Member of Parliament disgusted him. He was not interested in becoming a lecher, nor in drinking to excess. These were what brought many of the gentry to the point of bankruptcy. Their grand inheritances in land were also prey to the uncertainties of harvest and climate. There might be outbreaks of disease amongst their animals. Even the willingness of tenants to pay what they owed could not be relied upon. It was men of this class, like the eighth Earl of Pentelow, who most often called Foxe to help them sell books. Only thus could they stay out of the hands of their creditors.

Foxe's principles of investing were simple. He put his money into things people needed regardless of circumstances. He also kept a close eye on all who handled money on his behalf.

For the first principle, he turned to solidly-built properties. His favourites were buildings occupied by merchants, members of the professions and well-to-do people of the middling sort. He owned several such in Norwich itself, though not one of his tenants knew their landlord's identity. Both Kitty and Gracie Catt lived in houses he owned. So did nearly a dozen of the lawyers, doctors, merchants and prosperous shopkeepers of the city. He was owner of a major share in a brewery and maltings. With his friend Brock, he was a silent partner in a fine fleet of barges and Norfolk wherries. He had also bought a good amount of government securities and placed significant deposits with the prime bankers of the locality.

The second principle was equally simple. He kept his holdings local, so that he could watch over them in person and he employed committed Quakers as his agents and clerks whenever he could. Such people had the best reputation for honesty. Their modest style of life rendered them nearly immune from the main causes of fraud and peculation – gambling, whoring and indulging in strong drink.

His own lifestyle, though grandiose for someone who claimed to be a mere provincial bookseller, was also relatively modest. Thus his fortune was still increasing. His only significant indulgences were the Catt sisters and he took good care that they above all should not suspect the true extent of his wealth.

That day Foxe was once again a simple bookseller and son of a local printer visiting an old family friend. A man who just happened to be the editor of one of Norfolk's principal newspapers.

He found Sebastian Hirons, the editor of the newspaper, sitting surrounded by piles of journals, open books and handwritten notes. How the man ever found anything on his desk, or made sense of what he did find, was a rare mystery. Still there was little that passed in the city of Norwich that escaped his eye, even if he took care that much of it should not appear in his newspaper. Those who bought copies would not care to find too many of their personal dealings amongst the stories they read over their breakfast things or in the coffee house.

'Hello, young Foxe,' Hirons said when he noticed him. 'What do you want to know this time?' He was not a man given to polite pleasantries when they were not essential.

'Hello Hirons. Who says I want to know anything?'

'You wouldn't be here otherwise. I'm a busy man. Tell me what it is and I will give you the answer, if I know it. Otherwise go back to peddling old books and leave me to get on with bringing out the next edition.'

'Bonneviot,' Foxe said. 'Why was he laying off out-workers when the other master weavers seem to be prospering as rarely before.'

'Easy! Bonneviot had picked one fight too many with the London merchants who bought his cloth. All determined not to do more business with him. That left a huge hole in his book of orders and large stocks in his warehouse.'

'No more than that?'

'Wouldn't you say that was bad enough? The vast majority of shipments of this city's worsteds and other fabrics go to London. If you can't sell them there, where are you going to sell them?'

'Abroad?'

'Sounds easy, doesn't it, Foxe? Isn't though. You need contacts, agents, commercial travellers, heavy insurance and the ability to wait many months to get payment. Even the payment you do get will have passed through the hands of some banker. All such are eager to make money on changing a draft drawn on a foreign bank and in the local currency into English pounds. Bonneviot had none of these necessities in place. All his success had come from managing his costs, bullying his out-workers and negotiating with the London dealers.'

'Do you know what he was going to do?'

'I know what he wasn't going to do: eat humble pie and try to repair his reputation with those he had sold to before. Not his style. Bonneviot always had to win, whatever it cost him – or those around him. I suspect he was trying to find a way to open up new markets, in much the same way the merchants of Halifax and Bradford have done in recent years.'

'Could he have done that?'

'Maybe. Maybe not. Unless, of course, he found two things first.'

'Don't play with me, Hirons. You always did love to drag a story out. If you're so busy, get to the point and I'll leave you alone.'

'Bonneviot needed a banker willing to lend him a good sum. He also needed a partner with the knowledge and contacts to set up enough steady orders from around the country and abroad. The word is that he had found both. Before you ask, I have no idea who the banker was. The partner is easier. If I were you, I should look carefully at a certain Mr. James Hinman. Until recently, he claims to have been the right-hand man of a merchant in Halifax. Now he aims to set up on his own account in Norwich. I hear he is eager to find a source of cloth to sell in the countries bordering on the German Ocean.'

'So, Bonneviot supplied the cloth and Hinman supplied the knowledge and contacts and managed the sales. That might save Bonneviot's business. Is that the way of things?'

'I believe it may be.'

'What do you know of Hinman? Is he honest?'

'Probably as honest as most men who sell to others for a living. That is as much as to say devious, conniving and prone to exaggerating his prospects.'

'Nothing else?'

'Hinman only appeared in the city maybe three weeks ago. He seems wealthy enough to make a show in the coffee houses. He makes sure all should know of his plans and abilities. Yet I wager few of our sober master weavers would have given him the time of day. A regular braggart, many say. No, his problem was much worse than that.'

'Hirons! I declare you will drive me insane with your hints and prevarications. I am not some reader who must be tempted into turning the page. Speak plainly, I beseech you.'

'Hinman may be what he says he is. Only time will tell. What is far plainer is that he is a man in a hurry. He is, perhaps, closer in age to your tender years than my mature ones. Old enough to feel he should have made his fortune by this point in his life. Young enough to believe he may still do so, if he but moves quickly enough. Such thoughts make a man prone to every kind of rash action. It is my understanding that the Halifax merchants spent decades building up their overseas trade. Maybe Hinman convinced Bonneviot he could do the same here. Of course, Bonneviot was desperate, ready to believe anything that would offer him a way out of the morass he had put himself into.'

'So … Bonneviot takes Hinman as a partner in this new venture and tries to survive long enough to benefit from the results.'

'You have it in a nutshell. Have you ever thought of writing for a reputable newspaper?'

'Never! Nor, I am convinced, does such a journal exist. Now, is there more I must wheedle from you?'

'None whatsoever.'

'Then I will go and leave you to continue whatever you were doing.'

'Before you go …'

'Now comes the price!'

'I have heard tell that the Earl of Pentelow has amassed large debts through gambling. To pay them, he must sell his father's library. Are you dealing with those books?'

'The eighth earl is indeed desperate to raise money. Many could tell you so, not least his creditors, who will, I expect, have to wait a long time to receive even part of what he owes them. His father and grandfather were noted book collectors and the library at Pentelow Hall is renowned.'

'I'll take that to mean yes.'

'Take it as you will, Hirons. If you heard he is selling books, you cannot say you heard it from me.'

'Great God above! You are more slippery than a Jesuit lawyer.'

'And if you thought I would tell you ought of Lord Pentelow's books, you are more naive than a Bermondsey virgin. And only one of those has ever been found above ten years old.'

'Go away, Foxe. You got what you wanted.'

'As, I believe, did you.'

'Go away, I said.'

As Foxe left the editor's office, Mr. Hirons raised his head and called out, 'Who are you taking to the Mayor's Ball next month? Kitty or Gracie?'

Sadly, Foxe's hearing sometimes left much to be desired.

❧

Mr. Foxe wanted to go home. What was the use of this investigation? Each new piece of information added to the mystery. None of it made sense. He felt lost. What direction should he take next? Did it matter? The death of Bonneviot would probably never be solved.

But he had promised that he would visit Gracie Catt and could not disappoint her. Thus he walked with heavy step towards her house, looking neither right nor left. Even when Horton let him in, he ignored the man's friendly greeting and went at once to her room.

Gracie was waiting for him, all smiles – at least until she saw his face. 'Ash? What on earth …'

Foxe did not speak. He just gave her a perfunctory peck on the cheek and went over to the window. There he stood, frowning at the world outside but seeing nothing.

All the while, he was muttering to himself. 'Why kill …? Sure that would wreck all … Cannot have applied for probate either … Who are the executors …? Should have asked … Idiot! Where'd he get the money …? Why lend to a business in trouble?'

On and on he went. Behind him, Gracie walked to the fireplace and pulled the bell-cord to summon her maid.

'No interruptions on any account, Sally. Ask Miss Ruth to deal with any clients. I am not to be disturbed! And tell cook I will send to say when dinner should be ready. Until then, she is to wait. Now, be off!'

After a while, Foxe realised that all was silent in the room. He stopped his furious conversation with himself and listened. Not a sound. How rude he had been! And to Gracie too! In some apprehension about what his reception might be, he turned around.

The sight before him made him gasp. Gracie stood, waiting. On her head, she wore a simple lace mob-cap over her curls. For the rest, she was clad only in the lightest of shifts, so that he could see the nipples of her breasts resting against the fabric.

As he opened his mouth, ready to present the most abject apologies, she shushed him.

'Not a word, Ash! Come, take off your coat and waistcoat and put them here. Not a word, I said! I will help you with your breeches. Ah … I am glad to see that part of you at least remembers where you are. The shirt too must come off.'

All the while, she was urging him across the room towards a door open to her bedroom. When they were both inside, she pushed it shut behind her. Then she thrust her hands hard against his chest, so that he fell onto the bed rather than climbing into it. As he lay there, she removed her shift in one fluid movement and threw herself on top of him.

What passed next was but a blur of writhing, groaning and thrusting. Never had their passion been so intense. Never had they cried out so often as the longed-for consummation approached. When it was over, and they lay panting beside one another, it was Gracie who first found breath to speak.

'If that is the result of such a vile mood at the start, Ash, I give you permission to come to me every time your temper is bad. Now, my dear, listen well. I wish to hear nothing – nothing, I say! – about the matter of Bonneviot. Speak but one word about that and I will be gravely displeased.'

'But Gracie ...'

'No buts!' She wriggled against him, then giggled. 'What is this? Are you so soon recovered? Lah, sir, you are insatiable!'

This time, their love-making was more measured and gentle, though the results were much the same. What on earth the rest of the house would make of Gracie's squeals and his groans, Foxe could not imagine. But there, all within must be well used to such noises and what they signified. At least these were genuine. Most here were cleverly feigned.

Once more the two snuggled together, sweating now, but smiling too.

'Lie there,' Gracie commanded. 'I must rise and tidy myself a little before calling for Sally to come. No, lie still I say. Do not be troubled by thoughts of how the sight of you might offend her modesty. She has seen many a naked man. Though perhaps not so often one who, even now, is already almost ready for more.' She tapped the offending part of his anatomy with a finger.

Sally was summoned and entered grinning. Foxe had managed to cover himself with a sheet by this time and turned so that he presented a picture more of indolence than arousal.

Gracie gave her orders for dinner and told the girl to send word to Signor Vulpino's house that he would not be returning home until the morning.

When they were alone again, she looked down at her lover and shook her head. 'No, my dear. I will not return to bed, whatever pleading you offer. You may have other appetites, but my stomach is rumbling with hunger. Nor will it do to go to the dinner table looking as we do. But stay there a while and I will dress myself properly. Then you too must rise and become respectable again. Oh, my hair ...! I have no notion what became of the mob-cap, but my hair is entirely disordered.'

For Gracie, dressing was something to done to with the greatest care. Foxe had nearly an hour of rest before she returned, wearing a neat gown of dark-green worsted brocade over a petticoat of pale yellow, all dusted over with tiny flowers.

'Now, rise, sir! Sally has rescued your shirt and stockings from the floor and brushed down your coat. No need for a wig, but please make good use of the brush and comb I will provide. And before all, go to the washstand and make your face look less as if you have been ploughing in the fields.'

'But I was ploughing, Gracie dear, ploughing …'

'Enough!' Gracie laughed. 'Mind your manners, Ash. I will not have such coarse language in my house.'

Now Foxe was laughing too. 'I didn't know you made your girls entertain in the street outside, Gracie. That would be the only way to ensure that rule was never broken.'

Over dinner, they talked of trifles, sounding more like a happily-married couple of the middling classes than the madam of a bordello and her lover. Gracie thanked Foxe for the gift of fabrics for a new gown, praising both her sister's excellent taste and Foxe's liberality.

'I sent all to my dressmaker on the instant,' she said. 'She is to come early next week to discuss what she will make for me. She usually brings a mannikin too, so that I may see what she intends in drapes of the actual cloth. Once we have agreed, I may send for the hat-maker to produce something to finish off the ensemble.'

'I am sure you will be the most beautiful person present,' Foxe said. Then, remembering himself just in time, he added, 'Along with Kitty, of course. The two most beautiful.'

'Dear Ash. How good it is to see you restored to yourself. I wonder what could have lightened your mood so?'

'I have no idea,' Foxe replied. 'Maybe it was something you did.'

'I hope so, else it would have been a waste indeed.'

'Say not so! Such times with you … and your dear sister …' Foxe caught his mistake in time again. '… could never be accounted anything but the purest delight.'

'It is good of you to take us both to the ball, Ash.' Gracie was serious now. 'The old tabbies who make up the bulk of our Norwich society will tear your reputation to shreds for it.'

'I have little left to tear, so far as they are concerned. But you mistake both them and me. I would not have them leave disappointed. They account nothing so enjoyable as sharpening their claws by digging into some rich scandal. No, by taking the two of you I will quite make their evening.'

'Their husbands will have to hear of it for days.'

'They will not care. All, I imagine, are well used to assuming an expression of righteous disgust. The men will amuse themselves with thoughts of how they would have paid court to you both, were they but forty years less in age. If your dressmakers cut the necklines of your dresses low enough, I don't doubt all will have hurried to present their compliments to you both that evening. They will hope to catch sight of something to warm their bones better than their wives can.'

'You are such a cynic, Mr. Foxe.'

'I am a man, Miss Catt. It is what I would do in their places.'

'Fortunately for you, sir, you do not have to peer down a lady's dress. The ladies in question are both happy enough to show you all.'

'Though not, I declare, as happy as I am to see what they will show me. Now, Gracie dear. If you have eaten and drunk enough, I am quite fatigued. It would be of great assistance to my frail state to go early to bed.'

'Not too frail, sir, I hope.'

'We shall see.'

A third encounter followed, then both did indeed sleep. Foxe awoke soon after dawn. Gracie was still asleep beside him and he could not resist adjusting his position so that he could brush his lips once again across the soft skin of her breasts. That awoke her, of course, and nothing was to be done but to essay a fourth return to love's delights, but somewhat drowsily now.

None arose early in Gracie's house, for her girls must work until late in the night. No customers would return until the afternoon at least. Foxe and Gracie could sleep for a while longer, before the sounds of the house woke them and both started to consider breakfast a necessity.

That meal was also taken in a most leisurely manner, Foxe declaring himself to be 'quite … um … drained, I would say.' Nonetheless, he was not yet allowed to go.

'Signor Vulpino has been neglecting his duties to my girls.' Gracie said as they returned to her boudoir. 'Several have mentioned it to me. They are sure he must have found some other business to engage him.'

'Surely not! I should speak to the fellow most severely, madam.'

'Indeed, sir, though I would not hurt his feelings. These foreign gentlemen are apt to be far more sensitive that our bluff, English fellows. Besides, I am sure he will put in an appearance immediately the girls are ready for him this morning. And after that – and only after that – I will tell you the news you came for, but quite forgot in your … distracted … or would it be inflamed … state of mind.'

Foxe submitted to all with a good grace. Soon after midday, he joined the girls in the largest room in the house. There he put them through a testing lesson in walking correctly, sitting daintily and the finer points of dinner-table etiquette. A few sighs came at times, but none were ungrateful by the end. Indeed, Signor Vulpino had, as usual, to submit to many expressions of warmest thanks, and not a few kisses, before he returned to Gracie's room.

'Now, this is what my girls have learned for you, Ash,' Gracie said when they were alone together once more. 'You must not ask too many questions. I would not have you return to yesterday's most distempered state of mind.'

'Have no fear, Gracie. I have already determined that what I need most at this stage is to clear my head and come at things afresh. If you both agree, perhaps you and Kitty will do me the honour of walking with me in the gardens at The Wilderness one afternoon soon. Provided the weather is fine, that is. Then you must both dine at my house. Mrs. Dobbins, my housekeeper, is a most excellent cook. Providing meals for one offers but little challenge to her skill. She will relish the chance to display her true abilities in the kitchen.'

'I accept, of course,' Gracie said.

'Then I will send word to your sister.'

'Do not trouble yourself, Ash. I am to dine with her this evening and will carry your invitation. I have no doubt she too will accept.'

Kitty must already have heard that Foxe had spent nigh two days with her sister and would be agog for the details. Then, her own expectations raised, she would demand equal treatment. Such were the drawbacks of Foxe's most unusual liaison.

'So,' Gracie began. To business.'

#

'My girls like me,' Gracie said. 'I make sure they receive a good portion of what their clients pay. I feed and clothe them well. Thus, when I need their help, they work hard to provide what I want. That is true in this situation, Ash, believe me. Yet what they have found is, I fear, meagre fare.'

'Let them not be troubled on that account. I have been existing on a most niggardly amount of information from the start. Bonneviot seems to have trusted no one – nor liked any about him enough to confide in them. Whatever his plans might have been, they stayed locked in his head.'

'Very well. Let me begin with the Mr. James Hinman you asked about. There is a strange man. He came here but once, you know, and did not treat the girl badly – I would soon have the door barred against him if he did. He was also more than generous enough. Yet there was something odd about his behaviour. For a start, he did no more than ask the girl I paired him with to take off her clothes – all of them – and stand before him. Then he told her to dress and gave her a guinea. She said he seemed quite uninterested in her charms, but was a most tedious braggart. All the time she was with him, he talked of nothing save how rich he was. Then, after he was satisfied – if you can call it that, for he had not even laid one finger on her – he must needs begin again.'

'That does not surprise me, Gracie. What little I have heard of the man does not add to his credit.'

'She also told me he claimed to have come to our city to begin a venture that is going to make him a man of yet greater wealth. In his version of events, this will cause the Halifax men of business who turned him away to regret treating him with such scorn.'

So ... was Bonneviot the only master weaver Hinman had sought out? Was he the only one willing to believe Hinman's claims? That would not be so much of a surprise, if Bonneviot's business was already facing ruin.

'Whatever this venture may be,' Gracie went on, 'it has to do with trading in foreign parts. Hinman claimed to have spent many months overseas in the past and to be close friends with a long list of rich foreigners, even rulers. The girl thought he made it up to try to impress her, yet she could not see why. We get all kinds of men here, Ash. Not all are seeking to enjoy a woman in the usual way. Some have strange requests. Some want only to watch others do it. Some even pay a girl to pleasure herself, while they observe. Hinman was odd, but not so odd as to cause more than idle chatter amongst the girls. Most judged him probably more partial to boys than women. Perhaps he had come to try to scotch such rumours, or for a bet.'

'Yet that girl remembered him well, even though she must see a good many men in the course of a single day.'

'Well … yes. She was surprised that a man who seemed young and virile should not want to try a tumble with her. Requests to watch come mostly from those too old or frail to do more. Then there was the guinea – just for baring her body for a minute or less. Perhaps most of all, she remembered his constant boasting. He kept telling her he was Mr. James Hinman, that he was wealthy, and that she should remember him. One day, he said, she would wish to boast that he had spent time with her. When he was famous.'

Was Hinman telling anything near the truth about himself? He seemed to have money. Did he plan to start an undertaking in Norwich? That was how it appeared. He may not have such grandiose contacts as he claimed, but had he indeed spent time overseas? He must have caused Bonneviot to believe there were those amongst his former partners willing to trade with him again.

'Hinman had money from somewhere, or he could not have afforded to pay what I charged him,' Gracie said. 'Yet he never came again, so I judge his wealth is already much diminished. I did not think him to be a prudent man. To me he is a gambler. Not perhaps at the gaming tables, but certainly in business. And, I warrant, a gambler with other peoples' money too. So, there it is. All we could find on Mr. Hinman and little enough for our efforts.'

'Do not be down-hearted, Gracie. It may be small in extent, but it is worth a good deal to me. It confirms things I have heard elsewhere and offers me new directions for my search. God knows that I need them!'

'I have but two other pieces of information. See what you think of these. All my girls spend time with various of the master weavers of this city. Save for those who are Quakers, the rest like some variety beyond their wives. Some of these gentlemen are our most regular visitors. Now, it seems, the master weavers are much perturbed by Bonneviot's death. Not because they liked the man, but because they fear his business must collapse, to their own great discomfort.'

'How so? It would be one competitor fewer, and a significant one to boot.'

'They understand that his warehouses and storerooms are packed with unsold cloth. If it had to be sold quickly, say under terms of distress, they fear there is enough to depress prices for them all. Who will buy from them if he can get good cloth for far less outlay?'

'Of course!' Foxe said. 'They are right to be concerned. I expect all knew Bonneviot faced financial troubles. His death meant he could no longer escape them by means of future trades. His creditors must seize his goods and sell them at whatever price they can get. Only thus can they recover even a part of what he owed them. But why has that not occurred? Why are those storerooms still full?'

'I think my final piece of information may help you there. There is one master weaver, a Mr. Callum Burford, who comes here but rarely. His business is small and I doubt he has much money to spend on our kinds of entertainment. Yet he did come and but a few days ago. Like you, Ash, he was troubled and sought to lighten his woes in feminine company.'

'A most sensible man then. What do your girls say of him?'

'They like him, though he cannot afford great generosity. They say he is modest and kind. He does not boast. He does not claim to be other than he is. He always thanks them warmly for the pleasure they give him and seeks to give them pleasure in return. That, as you know, all are capable of feigning with great skill, so the man usually goes away well satisfied on both counts.'

'Do none within these walls find genuine pleasure in their bed-mates?'

'Do not fish for compliments, Ash. You might draw up nought but an old boot!'

'My apologies, Gracie. Pray continue.'

'Mr. Burford, as I said, is greatly troubled, for he is an honest man, unused to deception and sharp business dealings. Now, it seems, he was approached by Bonneviot with an unusual proposition. Though he agreed in the end, it was not without much searching of his conscience.'

'By Bonneviot! That I had not expected. I thought it was Hinman.'

'No, Bonneviot came to him some weeks back. As I am sure you know, Bonneviot had quarrelled with the London merchants, so that they would no longer do business with him. At first, Mr. Burford told my girl, Bonneviot had determined on selling his goods elsewhere. Then he seems to have repented of that idea and wished to sell to the Londoners again.'

'But all say he would never accept that he was in the wrong!'

'That was why he needed Mr. Burford's help. Burford was to act for him as agent in London. Mr. Burford had no trouble with the principal merchants there. Indeed, his reputation was good with all. Bonneviot offered him part of the profits, if he would sell Bonneviot's stocks of cloth alongside his own. That way, Bonneviot could avoid backing down in his quarrel and yet gain an income once again. For it appears he had approached several men in Norwich for loans and received a poor welcome.'

'I can see what was intended. So far as I can judge, nothing in the deal was illegal or even sharp business. Burford becomes an agent, sells

Bonneviot's cloth and they split the proceeds. The only unusual feature is that Bonneviot must keep his part in the deal a secret.'

'It is not the agreement which upset Mr. Burford. It is what he found on entering into Bonneviot's business. It was clear to him that the man had been trying to stay afloat by not paying his bills to those who supplied him with yarn and the like. Many of his out-workers had not been paid either, sometimes for many months.'

'Yes, I have heard the same.'

'Mr. Burford tackled Bonneviot about it. Bonneviot said a loan had now been agreed with a London banker. Soon there would be cash enough to pay the outstanding bills at least.'

'Did the cash come?'

'I do not know, for it was a little time ago that Mr. Burford was here. But would not Bonneviot's death render the loan re-payable?'

'I would have thought so. Oh, here is a fine mess! Gracie, my dear, I must think hard to sort it out.'

'Do not forget your resolution to clear your mind, Ash. Nor your invitation to me and my sister.'

'Indeed I will not! I will need the clearest of heads for this task. But one thing I do see, and it is most vital. I must warn the mayor and his colleagues at once that they face a crisis, both to the largest industry of this city and to its reputation. Once I have done that, I promise to set all aside until next week.'

'Go then and God speed!'

'Dear Gracie. As before, you and your girls have helped me in … shall we say … many special ways? I can reward you – and will – but your girls need a reward too. A small gift of money to the one who had to put up with Hinman, and the same to the one who entertained Mr. Burford. Perhaps two guineas apiece?'

'That is far too generous, my dear. Give such a reward and I will have every girl in the house pestering me with pillow-talk to pass on. A guinea between them would be ample.'

'Then I will give you the rest to use for treats amongst all the girls as you see fit. As you know, I strive hard to avoid favouritism.'

'You puzzle me greatly, Ash. Where does your money come from?'

'Frugality in my habits and a bookselling business that, though small, returns sound profits. Beyond that, you will look in vain.'

'Go! You may be a wonderful lover, but you lie woefully. Go, I say, before you shame yourself – and me – with such falsehoods!' But she was smiling as she spoke.

Chapter Ten

Disaster Threatens

ALDERMAN HALLORAN WAS DINING WHEN FOXE ARRIVED AT HIS HOUSE. But such was the seriousness of the message sent in to him that he left the table at once and came to his library, where Foxe was waiting.

Throughout Foxe's explanation of what he had found, the alderman sat in silence. Only the darkening colour of his face betrayed his emotion. That, and the way his hands gripped the arms of his chair, so that his knuckles grew white. When Foxe finally sat back to signal that he had no more to relate, there were several moments of silence as the alderman thought through what he had heard.

At length he reacted. 'Merciful God in Heaven! This could be a disaster for us all. I must go to the mayor at once! Are you sure of all this, Foxe?'

Foxe indicated that he was.

'If all that cloth were sold in the market at once,' Alderman Halloran continued, 'the price of finished goods would fall so low that no one else could trade, save at a terrible loss. Those without enough capital to hold off would have no choice. Nor could prices easily be raised afterwards. Our working men are difficult enough to hold in check at the best of times. With mass unemployment, who knows what they might do? Riot at least! The dyers and finishers too … And the yarn merchants …'

'Our whole manufacture would be affected,' Foxe said quietly.

'Nay, our whole city! Who would do business with us? All would be afraid of some other hidden scandal. Our bankers would sustain huge losses. Some of those too might fall into bankruptcy. No! Most of them, for cloth is our largest business and must account for many of their loans. Indeed, some are cloth or yarn merchants as well as bankers. The curses of all the demons of Hell upon Bonneviot! … The merchants of Halifax and Bradford will be overjoyed … aye, and those of Paisley … our downfall would be the finest present they could be given. It shall not happen, Foxe! By God, it shall not!'

There was silence again. Then Alderman Halloran sprang to his feet and hurried to ring the bell for a servant.

'This cannot – must not – be suffered! … Jenkins, tell my guests I must leave the house at once on most urgent business. Then summon me a chair and bring my coat.' He turned to Foxe again. 'Thank God you have been able to warn us in time, Foxe. We owe you a huge debt for what you have done.'

'You are going to tell the mayor?'

'On the instant! If we call the other aldermen together, there may yet be time for us to find a way to stop this disaster from happening. Leave all that with me, Foxe. We are men with significant power in this city on our own. If we act together, I believe none can stop us. What will you do next?'

'I am not certain, sir. As soon as I realised what might happen, I came to you at once. I have not yet had time to consider further moves. My best course, perhaps, will be to concentrate on extracting some more details of this situation. Let us hope that they point to whoever is behind it.'

'I leave all with you, Foxe. Succeed and I vow you will not lack for reward. But be discreet, I beg of you. None of this must ever be known outside the smallest group possible. All business stands or falls on trust. Once that is lost, it may never be recovered.'

'One more thing, Alderman, if you will indulge me thus far. Will you ask the mayor to send word to the mayor of Halifax to enquire what is known there of this Mr. James Hinman? I do not know if he is behind it all, but I have yet to find another who better fits that role.'

'Yes, Foxe, I will ask him. The man intrigues me as well. Besides, we have no need to accept men from outside our city into our dealings. I'm sure the mayor will agree with me.'

'The chair is here, sir. And here is your coat and hat.' Jenkins was back in the room.

'Farewell, Foxe. My thanks again. I will let you know what transpires.' And with those words, the alderman was gone.

What was he going to do? As Foxe returned to his home, he was thinking hard. Was this a plot to destroy Bonneviot alone, or to use him to undermine the whole business in Norwich stuffs? How could he move on until he knew that? Yet how could he find out, when all remained so obscure?

He was tempted to abandon his earlier promise to Gracie and rush into action at once. The alderman had confirmed that Bonneviot's business and stocks were in as bad a state as Foxe had reckoned.

Perhaps he could tackle Bonneviot's foreman himself and either bribe or bully information from him. No, if he looked at the matter using reason, rather than giving way to his passions, it was clear there was little more to do now. All would better wait until Monday.

And yet … yes … there was one thing that should not wait. Brock had not returned with any report on McSwiggan. They must not let that ruffian slip away. There was another matter too that Brock could help with.

Thus it was that Foxe put off his own dinner just a little longer, despite the frowns from Mrs. Dobbins. Instead he told Alfred to bring him paper and pen, then seek out the boy Charlie. A message sent by him would be bound to reach Brock faster than one taking any other route.

The requests that Foxe made in his message were these. First, if Brock had found McSwiggan, he should be watched every moment, however many men this required. But none should approach him save a single, most trusted person. That man should find a way to place himself in McSwiggan's company and ply him with drink. The object was to see if the man could be tricked into boasting of undertaking to kill someone for money. And whether he would tell who might have employed him in this way.

Take no risks, Foxe wrote, underlining the words, for it was much more important for Brock to keep McSwiggan from making off than to learn anything at this stage. When the time came, he had little doubt that between them they would find ways to loosen his tongue.

Foxe's second request was that Brock find a suitable group of trusted men to watch James Hinman, wherever he might be found. He was probably lodged at some inn in the city. Since he spent a good deal of time in the coffee houses, it should not be too hard for someone to follow him back to wherever he was living. Again, Foxe stressed that

Hinman must not be approached closely. It was vital he should not know any was taking interest in his movements.

He too must not be allowed to slip away. Money is no object in any of this. If you need twenty men, use them. Only – and this is vital – let no whisper of what you are doing reach Hinman's ears. I would not have him bolt before we can put into place the means to uncover his part in this affair.'

The last requests were the simplest, but perhaps the ones that would puzzle Brock most. First, Foxe asked him to send word by young Charlie, as soon as he could, that all was in place. That was simple enough. Then, he was told he must also send word, either at once or as soon as may be, of the names and addresses of the best forgers in the city. Foxe wrote that was not interested in those who forged coins or banknotes. The ones he needed to find were those who might forge a legal document and do it so well that none, unless they were alerted beforehand, would spot the deception.

Foxe now read over what he had written, sealed the note and called Alfred. 'Tell Charlie Dillon to carry this to Captain Brock at full speed,' he said. 'Promise to give him a whole sixpence if he can return within an hour to tell you it is in Brock's hands.'

Foxe was certain that what remained of Bonneviot's business must soon collapse. If that was true – and Hinman was involved somehow – he would be close at hand, keeping a careful watch on events. Their best hope would then occur when he had to come out of the shadows and stake whatever claim he had to part of Bonneviot's estate. It sounded simple, but Foxe knew that if Hinman realised he was suspected, he would probably make a run for it.

The letter written and sent, Foxe went in to eat and, afterwards, to sit and consider his next moves. Tomorrow he would concentrate on household matters and the demands of his neglected bookselling business. The next day, as he had promised, he would take the Catt sisters to walk in The Wilderness. They would enjoy the flowers and the company, before returning to dine on whatever fine dishes Mrs. Dobbins would prepare. During all that time, he would, so far as it was possible, forget about Bonneviot. Thus he would keep his promise to Gracie. That should give him the best chance of being able to set a course of action that would bring all to a speedy conclusion.

That the affair must end soon, he was sure. All that worried him was that it should not end with the escape of those who had set it in motion. Nor in a way that would bring harm to thousands of innocent people in the town.

Foxe ate without noticing the taste of the food, then sat in his favourite chair in his study. After another few minutes, Alfred brought word that Charlie had returned to claim his sixpence. All now depended on Brock. Though he did not doubt his friend, his mind would not be at ease until he knew the outcome.

Later, he realised he had no recollection of how he spent the rest of that evening, when he went to his bed or how long he lay awake when he got there. All was a fog, until he awoke to find the sun streaming through a gap in the curtains and Alfred quietly laying out his clothes for the day. No word had come from Brock, Alfred confirmed. Nor could Foxe make up his mind whether that suggested good fortune or ill. And so, still locked in uncertainty, Foxe allowed his routine to guide him during that morning.

Did any notice his state of distraction? He could not remember. Did they remark upon it? He did not know. He ate his breakfast, drank his usual dish of coffee without tasting it, looked at his usual newspaper and saw nothing, walked around the Market Place and had no idea who he passed or spoke to. All the while, his mind ran over and over the same problems and possibilities, testing, rearranging, retesting and always coming back to the same answer. He did not know.

Charlie at last brought a written message from Brock early in the afternoon. Alfred gave him tuppence, as usual, but the boy protested that the last errand had been worth sixpence. Besides, he had brought this one too at his fastest pace, so it ought to be worth the same. Gravely, Alfred said he would ask his master. He was affronted by the boy's cheek.

Foxe laughed and went to the door to speak with Charlie himself.

'I applaud your businesslike attempt to raise the price, boy, but I warrant you were not asked to apply unusual speed in this case. Now, tuppence is the rate for a letter in the city and tuppence it will remain. Yet here is a penny for your wit in asking. Now, be off, before I find another messenger who will offer me a better price.'

Taking the letter, he returned to his study. Should he read it at once? Would that break the promises he had made, both to himself and to Gracie? In the end, he decided that not reading it would produce too much anxiety. His attempt to clear his head and concentrate on other matters would be at an end.

Brock was, as usual, the soul of brevity. He wrote that he had done all as requested. They had found McSwiggan in a filthy lodging house and would not allow him to slip away. To get close enough to speak with him would need a strong stomach, since he stank like a midden, but it would not be hard to give him drink. It was likely all his money was gone. He would be desperate for any alcohol. Brock's man would do as Foxe had instructed.

Brock had also tracked Mr. James Hinman to an inn on the road towards Cromer. He was having him watched too. Should he try to slip away, Brock had enough men to follow him – and bring him back, if that was needed.

Next the counterfeiter. Brock could think of only one man able to undertake the kind of work Foxe specified. That was Joshua Underhill. He was once a clerk in a fine legal office. Then his taste for gambling on horse races caused him to develop the skill to produce forged letters of credit drawn on the partners' bankers. Nowadays, his business was writing letters and documents for those who could not afford the services of a proper lawyer. Brock was sure he had both the skill and the dishonesty to turn his hand to anything for enough cash.

Finally, Brock asked whether Foxe would expect him to visit him in the gaol when whatever deception he had in mind was discovered.

The man could never resist a clever remark, Foxe thought. Still, he had done all that had been asked and might be forgiven for it. Best of all, he had set Foxe's mind at rest. Provided the weather remained fair, the outing with Kitty and Gracie tomorrow should be a most pleasant affair.

Chapter Eleven

A Quiet Interlude

FOXE CONSIDERED THAT HE MIGHT FIT IN A SHORT VISIT to talk with the alderman on the subject of books before the polite time for taking dinner. That would not violate his promise to Gracie. The last time he and the alderman talked, there had been no occasion for any matter save the death of Bonneviot and its repercussions.

The alderman was, it seemed, dining with several other city dignitaries. Yet he could usually find a few minutes to talk books and that day was no exception.

'Must be brief, Foxe. My wife is almost ready and it will not do to keep her waiting or be late for our engagement.'

'I understand, Alderman. But I have here a list of authors some of whose works I could have for sale. If you could just cast your eye over it. Once I know which, if any, are of interest to you, I will bring the relevant volumes for you to examine.'

'Excellent, Foxe, excellent. Now, let me see … Dammit, man! Can't you write more clearly than this … Toland … No, not for me. More of a theologian or reformer … definitely a heretic … Desaguliers … Yes, much better. Most learned man. I'll look at any of his books. Now …' Thus he went on, thinking and talking at the same time.

In the end, Foxe had a short list of authors of interest. Desaguliers – what an odd name – Priestley, Black, Price, Kay. Newton too, of course, though Ald, Halloran said his books were 'deuced difficult to understand'. From an earlier time, Bacon, Hobbes and Locke. The alderman had added the names of several French authors whose books would also be of special interest to him.

'I couldn't make head nor tail of the writing in that book you left for me, Foxe. I suspect it's no more than alchemical gibberish. Still, I had occasion to pay a visit to the Master of the Dyers' Guild yesterday and left the book with him. I know he has all kinds of interests in chemistry and the like. Alchemy too, I shouldn't wonder. These dyers are close to being alchemists, if you ask me, with all their peculiar brews and concoctions.'

'Thank you, Alderman. I am most grateful. You're probably right that none of it means anything much, but I would like to be sure.'

'What was strange, mind you, Foxe, was how excited he became after he had done little more than glance at it. I wager he knows something about either the book or mind the notes. If you're lucky, I believe he might buy it from you at a good price. Don't want to tell you your business, but he's a rich man. You shouldn't let him get away with claiming it has little worth, then trying to buy it for a few guineas. You don't know him as I do. He's mighty sharp when it comes to money, I can tell you.'

'I will heed your warning. Now, I must delay you no further. I hope to be able to return in a week or so with several of these books for your approval.'

'Good fellow! Dinner is a social affair today, Foxe. Organised long ago. Still, a good many of the great men of this city will be present. The mayor should have been there too, but he has excused himself on the grounds of pressing business. I don't need to tell you what that is. Your discovery has set us all by the ears. Still, the mayor insisted I should keep this engagement in his stead, as you might say. When the ladies have withdrawn, I am charged with warning the others that trouble may be afoot. Then I am to request specific persons to set aside all other engagements to attend on the mayor and aldermen tomorrow. It is a bad business, Foxe. We must try to bring all to a conclusion as quickly as we may.'

'I agree, Alderman. I only wish I could report on further progress, but that is not yet possible.'

'Do not think I mean to put pressure on you. I told you purely to make clear that others are now active in this matter. One way or another, we may yet unravel this mess.'

Damn the man! It was, of course, too much to hope that the alderman would not raise the Bonneviot business. He could not know of Foxe's promise to Gracie. He was far more concerned that Foxe should not think he was planning to spend a convivial evening out when matters of such gravity lay unresolved.

In the event, the walk with Kitty and Gracie passed off successfully on all counts. The weather was fine and mild. The crowds in The Wilderness large enough to allow for the satisfaction of being seen by a good proportion of the middling and better sort of the city. Yet the place was not so thronged with people that it was burdensome in any way.

Foxe wore his newest suit in honour of the occasion. A frock coat fashioned from a pale blue brocade and decorated with a most elaborate filigree pattern in gold and silver thread. Breeches matching the coat both in shade and decoration. Silk stockings of the finest manufacture and shoes in dark blue, with a flowered pattern and silver buckles enriched with small diamonds, to complete the ensemble.

The Catt sisters had chosen their outfits with equal care. Not for them the over-decorated fabrics and towering hats, heavy with plumes and feathers of every type. Since both were blessed with uncommon beauty in their own right, they shunned anything which might suggest their looks relied more on artifice than nature. Thus their gowns were of simple design, though made of the finest materials – rich fabrics in the lustrous dyes for which the city was famed. Kitty shone in rich green to complement her tumbling auburn curls. Her petticoat was paler green Norwich calamanco, covered with a typical pattern of flowers. Gracie blazed in scarlet taffeta. This she wore over a petticoat of ivory calamanco decorated with golden roses. Even the most censorious ladies had little enough to criticise. Yet the two were assured that they would be the primary topic of conversation for several days to come.

Most of the gentlemen present regarded Foxe and his ladies with amazed envy. Those who were acquaintances of his went out of their way to present their compliments and thus be seen for a while in what had to be the best company out that day. Gracie and Kitty's far more numerous male acquaintances were less apt to greet them openly when their wives were present. Some, unable to pass without any acknowledgement, even contrived to assume an acquaintance with Foxe that was new to him. Others had to be content with furtive glances and the briefest of smiles, when they were able to catch one of the sister's eyes.

Dinner at Foxe's house matched the rest of the day in tasteful splendour. Mrs. Dobbins provided two courses of richly flavoured dishes light enough to allow the guests to sample a little of each. Alfred, at his master's instruction, first poured an excellent champagne. Later he brought wines from the pick of the hocks and clarets in Foxe's cellar. Since that was the finest cellar in the city, though few knew it, these wines would not have been out of place at the King's table.

Neither Gracie nor Kitty were prone to drink too heavily. When they all passed into the drawing room for tea and a few games of cards, they were cheerful and relaxed, rather than muddled in their speech.

Thus the time passed until the carriage, ordered by Foxe to convey the ladies to their homes, left shortly after midnight. For while neither lady need rise at an early hour, Foxe had received a note during the evening from Alderman Halloran. He was requested to wait on the alderman at ten o'clock the next morning. It sounded like a command.

Chapter Twelve

Bonneviot's Dilemma

WHILE HE WAS TAKING HIS BREAKFAST, Foxe heard someone come to the front door of his house and Alfred going to answer it. A few moments later, Alfred himself appeared, carrying a parcel that looked as if it might contain one or two slim books.

'That was the Earl of Pentelow's coachman, Master. His Lordship sent him to deliver this. It seems you asked for the records of some matter about His Lordship's books. The footman should have given them to you on your visit the day before yesterday, but he forgot the matter. Thus they have been brought today. There is also a letter with them.'

The Earl's letter was brief. These books contained the records of book purchases kept by his father and grandfather. He hoped they would be useful. Then he had added a further hope, this time that any second payment might be soon in his hands. Foxe suspected the two hundred pounds he had given the spendthrift earl had served to pay off only his most pressing debts.

There was not time today to look through all these records. Still, Foxe could not resist a swift perusal before he returned to more pressing matters.

The sixth and seventh earls had been meticulous record-keepers. They had listed each purchase, including the book titles, authors and the name of the seller. Some marks in a private code probably revealed the price paid, if you knew how to decipher them. How many books the two had bought! Foxe estimated there must be four or five thousand listed. Still, a library of the size of the one at Pentelow Hall could accommodate twice or three times that many with ease.

As Foxe's eye skimmed the pages, he stopped, stared and read more closely. Then he turned to several further pages. On each, he ran his finger down the lists of sellers and sometimes muttered under his breath. After some minutes of this, he straightened up and called for Alfred.

'Send young Charlie to find Brock. Tell him it is not urgent, mind, or he will be seeking a greater reward than usual.' Foxe smiled. He had little doubt Charlie Dillon would grow up to be something of a rogue. Little doubt either that he would be a damned engaging one. 'He is to ask Brock to call on me this evening, if he is able. Perhaps he should suggest he comes for supper. There is something I wish to show him.' As he finished his breakfast, Foxe hummed a little tune. Maybe matters were becoming clearer at last.

❧

While Foxe had been enjoying the sunshine and his delightful female company, it must have been a busy weekend at the City Hall. Alderman Halloran looked tired and pale when Foxe was shown into the library of his fine home in Colegate later that morning. He sat slumped in a chair, staring off into the distance and muttering under his breath.

'Ah, morning, Foxe. Coffee? I know that's your usual drink at this time of day. Pull the bell, there's a good fellow, and I'll get some sent in. By God, I am near too tired to get up from this chair. Up until all hours. Still, I think we've got everything sorted out. Sit down and I'll tell you what we have agreed.'

Foxe sat. The maid came, already bearing coffee, and poured each of them a dish of it. Then the alderman began.

'I don't know how much you understand of the weaving and cloth trade, Foxe. Those who run their businesses well can make good profits, but even they are prey to the whims of London fashion. Let a design be but six months old and many mercers deem it out-of-date and sell what stocks they have for cut prices. Master weavers, even the most successful, must needs walk a fine line. They must keep their out-workers busy by purchasing ample supplies of yarn. That demands good credit and the ability to pay promptly. At the same time, they must get enough orders to ensure the finished cloth leaves their warehouse quickly. The buyers expect credit, of course, so the master weaver must balance payments coming in with those going out. If they get it wrong, they soon find themselves without the money to pay their workers or buy fresh stocks of yarn.'

'I see,' Foxe said. 'They must be clever with money as well as with designs and cloth.'

'Indeed. Yarn merchants like myself are also at the mercy of ever-changing demands. That is why some are already looking to changing their businesses from selling yarn to banking. The Gurneys, for instance.'

'I had heard that too.'

'Besides that, we all rely on out-workers. Those in Norwich are most prone to riots and other disturbances if they do not receive what they believe is due to them.'

'Norfolk folk are well known for being disputatious. From the time of old Oliver, they have ever been amongst those most prone to take a stand against any who would try to compel them to obedience.'

'That is very true. Now ... Bonneviot was in a fix. He needed more credit to survive his foolish falling out with his buyers in London. But he could not get extra finance in Norwich. All knew of his quarrel and the difficulties this would make for his business. He had also gone just about as far as he could in delaying payments to his suppliers and out-workers. The suppliers were loathe to give him more credit and the weavers were damned close to burning his house down.'

'He was desperate.'

'He was.' The alderman sighed several times. This was matter that he must have rehearsed many times during the past two days. Foxe waited for him to go on.

'Now, we all agreed that Bonneviot's business cannot be allowed to collapse in a period of panic. It will be wound up, of course. No doubt about that. The need is to do all in an orderly manner. His debts must be paid to workers and suppliers. His cloth must be sold in the normal way of business – or as much of it as can be – so that the general prices of our stuffs are not affected. That requires extending credit.'

'From London?'

'No! They have no interest in the stability of our trade. The London banker whom Bonneviot persuaded to give him a loan will want to pull out of the deal the moment he hears of the man's death. We do not know if he has advanced any money already. In many ways, we hope that is not the case. If he has, our London friend will be at the head of the queue of creditors. The only way any of them will receive anything is the way we most want to avoid. An immediate auction of

Bonneviot's large stocks of finished cloth for whatever price they can get.'

Foxe sat silent. He had already surmised much of this, but he did not want to hurry the alderman through his explanation.

'This is what we have decided, Foxe. A consortium of local bankers and merchants have agreed to provide whatever credit is needed. That will make sure the out-workers get their wages and the accounts of yarn merchants and finishers are paid. If the Londoner has lent money, we will ask to take over that loan. If not, he may be ignored.'

'A sensible solution, sir. I have one suggestion to add, but I would not interrupt you now. We will come back to it.'

The Alderman frowned, but continued. 'Mr. Callum Burford has been seen by the mayor and the Master of the Weaver's Company. They have prevailed upon him to keep to his role in disposing of the stocks of cloth Bonneviot had built up. Certain people will assist him to see this is done in an orderly manner. If it goes well, all our loans will be repaid in time. If some are not, that will still cost us less than a collapse in our markets.'

The alderman paused and tasted some coffee, then pulled a face and set down the dish again. Foxe had already drunk most of his. The alderman's must be cold.

'So, to come to an end,' Alderman Halloran said. 'As he sells the stocks of cloth, Mr. Burford will repay the loans and the business will be wound up in stages. Burford's reward will be to incorporate the best parts of the business into his own firm.'

'At what cost to him?'

'That will be between him and the executors of Bonneviot's will. There will be little enough left for the widow at the end, I imagine. We have spoken with the lawyer handling the probate of the will. It seems Bonneviot had determined to treat his son as he himself had been treated. The son is left nothing. The widow gets the house for the span of her life, or until she remarries, and just enough to live on. The rest goes to various charities and hospitals. Bonneviot probably hoped to be more popular in death than he ever was in his life. Now, I doubt these good works will see much, if anything.'

'I feel sorry for the widow. The son, I gather, is something of a wastrel.'

'Yes, the widow may not be as well provided as she should have been. The son, I dare say, will either reform under the shock or go to the bad altogether. Better that, though, than the public disgrace of a bankruptcy – and a mass of creditors seeking to claim even the household goods to sell. The executors of Bonneviot's will have agreed this route is in the best interests of his estate. No trouble is expected from that quarter.'

'You have all worked hard, Alderman. I applaud your actions wholeheartedly.'

'Yet you said you had a suggestion.'

'It is this. I believe I know who may be behind this whole conspiracy. Yet knowing is not proving. It will not be easy to expose him to the law and obtain a conviction, since he has worked through others. He will, I expect, rather see them go to the gallows to save his own neck.'

'Can you catch him? I'm sure I speak for all the merchants of this city in saying I would love to see him dangle at a rope's end!'

'I think I can, with your help.'

'You have it! What must I do?'

'But one thing, for the present. Let Mr. Burford have just enough money to deliver the weavers from the extremity of want. Yes … and to pay those others Bonneviot has kept waiting longest. No more than that. He should put about a tale something like this. He has received payment from some account that has been outstanding for many months. Knowing the extent of the need, he is using the money from this to make partial payments. Whether there will be any more forthcoming, he cannot say.'

'None will be happy with this. They will assume the rest of what they are owed is lost.'

'I regret asking for this deception, but there is no other way. I need to flush the criminal into the open. For that, he must believe his scheme has succeeded. If the workers and other creditors are all paid in full, he will smell a rat. Then, as I judge, he will bolt from the city and all chance of bringing him to justice will disappear. No, sir, this is the only way. The more the word goes around that Bonneviot's business is about to fall into bankruptcy, the safer the villain will feel.'

'I don't know, Foxe. It took considerable persuasion to get everyone to agree to what I have told you. To ask them now to delay …'

'I ask you this most earnestly, sir. It will not be for more than perhaps two weeks at the most, perhaps less. Once we have our man, all debts may be paid in full as you have provided. And if he does not show himself in that time, he will not do so, so further delay will be useless. Just two weeks!'

'Very well, Foxe. Without your help, we would all be staring into the face of ruin. We owe you this much. I will get agreement to your delay, though I suspect I will earn some foes along the way.'

'I am most grateful, sir. Most grateful. Now, I will be off to ensure the rest of my trap is set. Please give the mayor my best compliments, Alderman. Tell him I hope soon to have work enough for his sword-bearer and the constables.'

'The sword-bearer? Then you expect to point him towards criminals to be arrested and brought before the court? That is his role in the city's affairs.'

'I do, sir.'

The alderman looked happier for the first time that morning. 'That will make them agree to your delay, I warrant. If the mayor, in his role as magistrate, may anticipate seeing the rogues who ruined his weekend standing in the dock before him, he will agree to anything.'

As Foxe went to leave, the alderman touched his sleeve. 'Could you spare a few moments to speak with the Master of the Dyers' Guild, Foxe? He's waiting in the small parlour and is most eager to ask you something about those books you left with me.'

Foxe nodded his assent and a servant was sent to bring the Master to the library.

Chapter Thirteen

Norwich Worthies

SAMUEL WERRETT, MASTER OF THE NORWICH GUILD OF DYERS, was a small man. Yet his meagre stature in no way reflected his importance in the affairs of the city. The Norwich Dyers and Hot Pressers were essential to the success of the worsted trade. The richness of the colours they could produce, coupled with the sheen or moiré patterns made by hot pressing, gave Norwich stuffs one of their main attractions to buyers. Other woollens were fulled and felted, giving a thick, somewhat heavy cloth. Norwich men made worsteds from mixed yarns, with the pattern of weaving still visible. And where some cloths were woven first, then dyed a single colour, each yarn used in Norwich weaving was dyed before the weaver set it on the loom. Thus Norwich stuffs abounded in stripes, flowered patterns, brocades and damasks. The dyers also produced many dark colours, hard to achieve elsewhere. The rich, lustrous black of Norwich bombazines, for example, made them nearly essential for mourning wear amongst the better classes.

After affable greetings, Master Werrett came straight to the point. 'I want to buy this book, Mr. Foxe. Now, I could try to play tricks with you, pretending I have no interest to make you lower the price. I will not. Halloran here tells me you are an honest man whom I can trust to deal fairly.'

'I believe I am, Master Werrett. It is important to me to have customers who will recommend me to others. That is worth more than to make a few extra guineas, while earning a dark reputation.'

'So I have heard. Now, let me tell you what you have here and why I will pay a fair price for them. The book itself, as you no doubt guessed, seems of little value. I do not know. I have no interest in alchemy. It is the annotations which I will pay for.'

'I have come to the same conclusion as you, Master Werrett. Books on alchemy are seldom valuable today. Yet your interest in the annotations intrigues me. Annotations in a book generally reduce its worth, unless they record the thoughts of some famous person. I will be honest with you, sir, as I hope you will be with me. On the face of it, this book, from an incomplete set, is worth barely four or five shillings. Maybe less.'

'I appreciate your openness, Mr. Foxe. Now, let me explain why these particular annotations may be of much greater worth.'

It was as Foxe had by now suspected. Master Werrett explained that the receipts written by hand into the book were for making various colours of dyestuffs. Some of them must be more than a hundred years old, handed down within families of master dyers. Such men defended the secrets of their trade with notable fierceness. That might be why these had been concealed by writing them on free pages and spaces in a printed book. Few dye receipts ever became available outside the original family. Indeed, it was the near-invariable custom for any written records of dyestuffs to be destroyed, if there was no son to inherit them.

'From the languages used,' Master Werrett said, 'these must relate to a Huguenot family. The family lived at first in some place where they spoke French. Then they moved – perhaps on marriage – to Flanders or the Spanish Netherlands, and finally to England. The family's dye receipts were written down in this book and passed from generation to generation. At last, the family changed their business so the book was no longer valuable to them. I am surprised it was not burned, but there you are. Did you obtain it from someone associated with the cloth trade?'

'Not at all, Master. I am puzzled how it might have come into the hands of the person who has now asked me to handle a discrete sale of certain volumes. Indeed, I suspect he has no idea he owns it, nor the other that goes with it …'

'There is another volume, annotated like this one?' Master Werrett's excitement was plain.

'Indeed so. I have both. Since I did not know what they were or might be worth, I left one with Alderman Halloran to seek his counsel.'

'Both are for sale?'

'Perhaps. The owner has given me a free hand to choose books to sell for him. I have promised to select the smallest number that will provide him with the sum he requires.'

'Name your price, sir!'

'It is not quite so easy, Master Werrett. You have trusted me and I will not betray your trust by raising my price to some giddy level, simply because I sense your eagerness.'

'I am eager, Mr. Foxe. The reason is simple. I judge these receipts to be concerned with the dying of silks and to contain shades we have not known exactly how to reproduce. Any dyer would be eager to lay his hands on them. Used well, they might bring him great reward. He would also want to be sure that they should not fall into the hands of a competitor. There, now you know all.'

'Thank you, sir. But I still lack one piece of essential knowledge. You say that they might bring commercial rewards. How great? The worth of the receipt must depend in large part on the value of what might be made from it.'

'I see you are indeed a man of business, Mr. Foxe. Now, I cannot give you a plain answer. I have had little time to peruse these receipts or try any out. You have also told me there is a second book. Does it contain a similar range of shades and types of dyes? Are more or fewer already known to us?'

'Yes, I see the problem. Well, let us help one another. You have trusted me by helping me understand the true worth of what I have here. I will trust you by sending the second book to your house. Then I will allow you time to examine both and estimate what they may be worth to you and your business, before making an offer. I will let you tell me a fair price, sir, and will sell them to you for that amount.'

'My good sir, you do me a great honour! Be assured I will not betray you. But send me the other book and allow me a week to consider what they contain and I will set as fair a price as I can – aye, and pay it willingly.'

'You have made a friend there, Foxe,' the alderman said after Master Werrett had left. 'I have known Werrett for many years. He is both honest and fair in his dealings. Indeed, I imagine he will be so eager to prove that he has not cheated you that the price he sets will be a high one.'

'So I judged, Alderman. I must be fair to my client as well. He too is trusting me. Now, with your permission, I will take my leave. I have much to think about.'

'You haven't got hold of some books from a family in the cloth trade, have you Foxe? Some large clan with past interests in dyestuffs as well as yarn or pressing? Huguenots, Werrett guessed. That would make sense, especially since he thought the dyes were for silk. A family from Smithfield originally?'

'It is no good, Alderman. I will not let slip anything about my client in this matter, however hard you try to tempt me. Be content that I believe I will have some books to offer you in a few days that I am sure you will like. Now, good day to you, sir. Thank you for your help in this matter. I will not forget, though you know me better than to believe my gratitude will be reflected in the prices I ask. Still, I may just bring one or two books to you first, rather than offer them to others I think might be willing to pay more.'

'Foxe …' But the alderman's guest was gone.

Foxe did not go home when he left the alderman's house. Instead, he turned east a little and sought out the premises where his friend, Nathan Hubbard, did business as a lawyer. He would now be in his office, though he might have someone else with him already. If so, Foxe would arrange a convenient time to call later. He needed a piece of information a lawyer would be best placed to give. But only one he could trust to stay silent afterwards.

Once again, luck was with him and Mr. Hubbard agreed to speak with him right away.

'What has brought you to my office, Foxe? I warrant you need some information! I have never known you to make a social call on anyone, without some hidden motive in your mind.'

'Good morning, Hubbard. You are correct, of course. I do need information. But I also need your promise to say nothing to anyone about what I must ask. Secrecy is vital in this matter.'

'When was it not, with you? And when have I ever blabbed?'

'True enough, my friend. I do not doubt you, or I would not be here, but I must say it just the same. I'm sure you will have wit enough to work out the matter that engages my attention at present. It is coming to a head and even the smallest slip may yet ruin all.'

'How do you get involved in such things, Foxe? You are – or claim to be, for none knows with you – a simple bookseller.'

'I am indeed a bookseller, Hubbard, as you know very well. As for simple – no, I never claimed that.'

'Just as well, or you would be foresworn twenty times over and more. Now, I am a busy man today, so come to the point.'

'Suppose you were party to a conspiracy to bring someone's business to ruin, then step in and secure it for yourself at no cost. What documents would you need to have had forged?'

Mr. Hubbard sat back in his chair, his mouth open and an expression of complete shock on his face.

'What...? Forged...? I would never...! This trumps all, Foxe. Do you take me for a criminal?'

'Not at all, friend. Just a most careful and experienced lawyer. Imagine if you had a client who had just died and whose business seemed likely to be falling into bankruptcy. Many creditors are waiting to place a claim on the estate – yourself included. Then a person comes along and says that the whole stock and business is his, sold to him before the man died.'

'Bonneviot! I should have known you must be meddling in those murky waters! Is that the way of it then?'

'I said you would be clever enough, did I not?'

'Right! I see how to answer you now. I need not concern myself that you have somehow either decided to become even more of a rogue yourself or make me out to be one. Well…in the first place, is this supposed buyer a master weaver of this city?'

'Let us say that he is not.'

'Then his scheme is over before it is begun. Let him have a mountain of documents to prove his ownership of Bonneviot's business and it will be of no use to him. The Company of Weavers would never allow anyone not possessing the freedom of this city to do business here. His purchase, even if it were fair and legal otherwise, would be worthless.'

'Hmm…perhaps I am on the wrong track after all. Is there nothing that might be of use to him in claiming to own such a business?'

'Well, let me think. Not if he wants to carry it on here. Nor would it be possible to do so elsewhere, unless he has the freedom of another place like Bradford, or Halifax, or Paisley. He could not even sell any stocks of finished cloths in this city…'

Foxe sat upright at that. 'And outside? Could he sell the stocks outside?'

'I imagine he could. If he could prove he owned them, he could sell them just as any mercer or intermediary might do.'

'Overseas? London?'

'Most certainly. Nearly all the trade in Norwich stuffs passes through the hands of London intermediaries.'

'So he would not need to lay claim to the business, just the stocks of unsold cloth.'

'That's right. Though few master weavers hold large stocks in their warehouses. A stock of materials is already going out of fashion and is worth nothing until it is sold.'

'But if this man believed his prey did hold large stocks, and those of recent manufacture?'

'Then, if he obtained them by fraud rather than purchase, he would stand to make a fortune.'

'And what legal documents would he need to prove his ownership?'

'Nothing but a proper bill of sale, signed and sealed before Bonneviot's death, of course.'

'That is the answer! I knew I could rely on you, Hubbard.'

'Even were such a document genuine, he might expect every lawyer working for the creditors to subject it to most careful scrutiny. It would deprive their clients of most, if not all, of the funds that might otherwise settle their debts. If it were to be a forgery, it had better be a convincing one.'

'Indeed it would. And I imagine our man knew that. If I am right, he went to see the best forger in the city. One whose documents already reside in many a lawyer's strongbox – even yours, I dare say.'

'Do not say so, please, not even in jest! Every lawyer lives in fear of encouraging a client to rely on documentation produced to support some claim, only to find that it is a forgery. Who is that forger? If you know his name, let him be brought to justice at once, I say!'

'Calm down, Hubbard. I assure you that, if all goes as I plan, the man will not be a trouble to any of your profession in this city in the future. As for the past, who can say?'

'May God guide your hand then! Now, I beseech you, give me no more shocks of that kind. There is only so much a man can take on a Monday.'

'Fear not! Only keep silent and I will rid you of this rascal – and, if I can, the man who hired him. Now I must fly, for there is much to do in a short time and all depends on it. Be of good courage, Hubbard, and stay silent, I beseech you. Then all may yet be well.'

Chapter Fourteen

A Conspiracy Unmasked

'I DON'T KNOW, FOXE. ARE YOU SURE YOU AREN'T MAKING THINGS WORSE?' Evening had come at last. Brock and Foxe had first taken supper together. Now they sat in comfortable chairs in Foxe's study. Naturally, they were talking over the matter of Bonneviot.

Brock looked at his friend and shook his head. 'Run through this business about the books again for me.'

'I'm almost as confused as you are, Brock. Let's start with the facts. The sixth earl, the current one's grandfather, bought various books from Jerome Bonneviot, Daniel's father. Jerome must have been the book collector. He sold books from time to time in the way all collectors do – to make room and raise cash for more.'

'But I thought Jerome Bonneviot was a Calvinist. Now you say 'e collected books by alchemists, freethinkers and heretics.'

'The one doesn't necessarily rule out the other, Brock. We know he was religious in his old age and just assumed that was the typical Huguenot Calvinism. Perhaps it was not. Perhaps he allowed people to believe he was a Calvinist as a way of deflecting too great an interest in his true inclinations.'

'Perhaps if I goes outside they'll be pigs flyin' around the cathedral steeple!'

'Only if you drink much more than you have so far, Brock. Be serious! Jerome Bonneviot sold a small number of books of that kind to the sixth earl. That doesn't make him some kind of wild heretic himself, any more than it makes one of the earl. He may have been curious. He may have believed in knowing your enemy.'

'Then Daniel sold the rest of his father's books to Pentelow Hall, you said.'

'Yes. Well, most of them, but over time as he needed money. He sold a few to the sixth earl – who was by then an old man – and more to the seventh. He also sold books in groups, sometimes of many volumes. My guess is that he had little or no interest in his father's collection. To him, they were a convenient source of cash whenever he needed it. I imagine the sales helped him extend his business or avoid taking on debt to do so.'

'And these two books Master Werrett is so mad about?'

'Daniel sold them to the seventh earl about two years ago, as part of a large group of books on alchemy. It looks as if Daniel didn't recognise them for what they were. Maybe he didn't even open them first. The seventh earl simply found them amongst the group.'

'Did the earl know what 'e had bought?'

'I doubt it. I imagine he found two books forming an incomplete set. That's what happens when you buy a large number of books at one time. You always run the risk of getting a few you don't want. So he tucked them away on that top shelf out of sight until he could decide what to do with them.'

'So … I've been patient, Foxe, but I can't see why you think all this 'as anything to do with Daniel Bonneviot's murder.'

'Suppose Daniel did have the third volume. Suppose he even had other notebooks of dyers' receipts and secrets. Master Werrett thought the book I showed him contained notes made by a Huguenot family … a family like the Bonneviots. The Bonneviots were weavers – at least in recent years – but might they have had relatives who were dyers; or been dyers themselves, sometime in the past. According to Master Werrett, some of these receipts must be more than a hundred years old. Perhaps Daniel Bonneviot recognised the other receipts he has for what they are. He may have missed these, because they were written in books he never opened. Now, we know of late he needed money badly. What better than to sell whatever other receipts he has for something closer to their real value. Besides, the seventh earl was dead. The eighth has no interest in buying books, I assure you.'

'And …'

'Say Bonneviot tries to sell his other dyers' receipts – or some of them – to someone else … say Hinman. Why not? But Hinman decides to get them free, as well as the cloth. He calls Bonneviot to a meeting, pays McSwiggan to slit his throat and takes the notebooks.'

'There's a terrible lot of supposes, guesses and imaginings in that. In the end, it still comes down to McSwiggan bein' the killer and Hinman the one who paid 'im. Gets us no further, if you asks me.'

Foxe looked miserable. 'When you put it like that …'

'Unless, of course, there were two plots. In the middle of Hinman tryin' to get the cloth, Bonneviot tries to sell 'is books to someone else and gets murdered as a result. That makes Hinman a cheat, but no murderer.'

'My head aches! I was so sure I had it right. Now I may have been right and wrong at the same time.'

Foxe put his head in his hands in such a comical expression of despair that Brock had to laugh. 'Serves you right,' he said. 'Keep things simple, I says. Anyhow, I'm for my bed. Thank you kindly for supper, Foxe. You'll puzzle it out. You always do.'

Foxe had to admire young Charlie Dillon. The boy had sensed some important matter was afoot and there could be a good number of errands as a result. According to Alfred, he had been hanging around close to Foxe's house for most of the day. Now his patience and persistence were about to pay off.

The day had begun with Foxe's usual trip to the coffee house, followed by a walk around the Market Place. But as soon as Foxe arrived home, he told Alfred to dispatch Charlie to find Brock and summon him to the house as quickly as possible. It was important that they planned the next stages of this affair with the greatest care. Timing would be crucial. And with so much to be done in the space of a day at most, Foxe would need Brock's help.

When Brock arrived, Foxe took him into the parlour and called for a jug of punch to be brought. Then, while he served Brock with the drink, he ran through again what they had learned so far. When he finished, Brock grunted his approval and waited for what would come next.

'There are, as I judge things, only three people involved in this conspiracy,' Foxe said. 'McSwiggan carried out the murder. The forger, Joshua Underhill, produced the necessary document. Mr. James Hinman is the mastermind behind it all.'

'No extra person buying receipts for dyestuffs?'

'No … at least, I don't think so. If there is, we'll find out when we question McSwiggan. Until then, I'm following your advice to keep things simple.' Brock grunted as before, so Foxe continued. 'Hinman's plan is to use his forgery to claim ownership of Bonneviot's large stocks of finished cloth. Thus he will pay nothing and sell them at a huge profit. At the beginning, he may have envisaged a genuine partnership with Bonneviot. I do not know. Then, somehow, he discovered that Bonneviot was planning to back out of the deal. In his anger, he decided on this new plan. It would allow him to make a vast profit and punish Bonneviot at the same time for his treachery. I suppose it might even have been his plan from the start. Hinman uses people to serve his own ends. He has no interest in them beyond that.'

Foxe paused to drink his punch. Since Brock was still silent, he pressed on. 'What I think he has not found out about – Hinman I mean – is the action by Bonneviot to take out a loan to keep his business going on its own; nor the agreement with Mr. Burford to sell the stocks of cloth on Bonneviot's behalf. If he had, he would have acted by now. As it is, he's in no hurry.'

'Why's that?' Brock asked.

'Hinman is cunning, but careful too. As matters stand, there is nothing to connect him with Bonneviot's murder. He can acknowledge the proposed partnership and portray himself as just another one of the many people that Bonneviot has cheated and left with debts unpaid.'

'What about the other creditors? Won't they want to sell Bonneviot's stock to raise money to settle their debts?'

'Assuredly. But if Hinman came forward too quickly, it might look suspicious. He will wait until all the creditors are invited to present their claims. His believes his forged documents will give him the stock in spite of them. Remember, it purports to show that Bonneviot sold all the stock to Hinman well before his death.'

'When will he make his move?'

'If I can bring things off as I wish, he will do so at a time of my choosing.'

'Right,' Brock said. 'What's the plan and what's my part in it?'

'First we have McSwiggan and Joshua Underhill arrested. We need to do that as quickly and as secretly as possible. I don't think it will panic Hinman into making a run for it, but I don't want to take the chance either. It would make him nervous though and I want him to believe that he can act boldly when the time comes.'

'D'you think either would testify against Hinman?'

'It's up to us to ensure that they will. We may be able to bring him to a successful trial without their help. Yet it would be far easier if we could produce their evidence to back up our assertions that Hinman is behind it all.'

'Persuasion?' Brock frowned and bunched his fists. 'I doubt McSwiggan will be much problem. We think 'e's already drunk all his money. Give 'im another day or so without grog and 'e'll agree to anything for a single taste. Underhill, the forger, is another matter.'

'I expect so. We'll visit each of them together. If you're right about McSwiggan, the main thing will be to frighten him enough to make him keep his word. I'll speak to the alderman. We may be able to promise to save McSwiggan's neck if he turns King's Evidence. Transportation instead of hanging.'

'Either way, 'e'll be dead soon enough,' Brock said. 'He'll find some way to get 'is grog, even in the gaol. The state he's in, it won't take much more to send him into eternity.'

'As you said, the forger will be harder. I may be able to offer him a way to avoid prosecution altogether, if he co-operates. Then it depends if he believes me.'

'Leave that to me,' Brock growled. 'I'll guarantee to make that kind of feeble pen-pusher see where 'is best interests lie.'

Foxe regarded his friend for a moment. They had known each other for many years and he knew he could rely on the older man for anything. Foxe also knew that Brock's rugged exterior hid a sharp mind and a good heart. Even so, the man was tall and powerful and not much given to tolerating opposition. To cross him in any important matter would be no small thing. No, the forger would definitely come off much the worst if Brock lost his temper.

'Very well. We may both need to apply our own methods of persuasion, Brock, since time will be against us. I wish to know I can rely on the witness of the other two conspirators before confronting Hinman. There seems to me to be little chance he will confess. He'll try to brazen it out to the end. What has he got to lose? If we gain a conviction, there will be no lessening of his sentence.'

'So … that's our plan. What first?'

'An advertisement in the paper asking all Bonneviot's creditors to present their claims to the lawyer handling probate. Meanwhile, be ready, Brock. If I can, I will induce Hinman to come forward almost at once. The instant he does that, we will have the other two seized and go to work on them.'

'Fair enough.'

'In the meantime, have the watch on each applied with even more care. None must escape, especially Hinman.'

Brock looked at Foxe and shook his head.

'I do not doubt you, friend. You know that. It is my anxiety about this affair that speaks, not my reason.'

'I know,' Brock said. 'Set your mind at rest. Those three can't take a pee without me knowing of it, much less leave the city. Can I go now?'

'It's not like you to be in a hurry, Brock.'

'I've got an hour before I must relieve one of my watchers, if you must know. I've also got my eyes on a frisky young mare who needs an old stallion. If I go now, there may be enough time to see 'er smile and still be on time to let my friend go home for 'is oats too. Good enough reason?'

'The very best!'

Chapter Fifteen

The Trap is Set

THE NEXT MORNING DAWNED FINE AND BRIGHT, but with a keen wind from the northeast. Not a day to make people stay indoors, but not one to tempt them to wander around Norwich's great Market Place any longer that they needed. The poor hurried to their hovels to stay warm as best they could. Working men were long engaged in their trades and would not venture forth again until the end of the day. And Norwich's complement of the better sort of people, together with a good many idle loungers, had mostly decided the best place to spend their time was, as usual, in the coffee house.

Alderman Halloran was already seated at a suitable table when Foxe arrived, precisely at ten o'clock as was his habit. The alderman was not such a constant customer of The Swan as Foxe, but he attended most of the better coffee houses from time to time, so his presence would cause no particular surprise.

Seeing an empty seat at the alderman's table – exactly as they had arranged the previous evening – Foxe made his way to sit there, showing no hurry. This was a man who had noticed an important business acquaintance and had decided to make use of the opportunity to either improve that acquaintanceship or do a little business. He had no need to order. The waiter knew exactly what he required and had brought it almost before Foxe had seated himself comfortably.

'Morning, Foxe,' the alderman said, trying hard to seem off-hand and sounding rather peevish as a result.

'Good morning, Alderman. I hope you are well. It is a fine day, but the wind makes it chill enough for winter. Seeing the sun from within, by a warm fire, is definitely better that walking outside, is it not?'

'Damn cold, if you ask me. Nor-easterly wind. Few ships will leave Yarmouth Roads today, I'll warrant.'

'Indeed not, sir.'

Thus they engaged in polite conversation of a totally innocent kind until the alderman could hold back no longer. Pushing a copy of the day's Norfolk Intelligencer across the table-top, he tapped a thick finger on a section in the right-most column of the front page.

'Seen this, Foxe?'

Foxe had, indeed, read the passage most carefully over his breakfast, but he returned the agreed answer instead. The alderman was not a natural actor. It would not be wise to force him to improvise his lines.

'Hmm …' Foxe read the brief notice with close attention. 'Bonneviot's estate … Do you think there will be many creditors eager to claim their share? I did not know the man, sir, but his business had a reputation for being one of the largest in the city.'

'You don't want to believe all you are told, Foxe.' Alderman Halloran's voice was naturally loud and deep. He had no need to speak more loudly to be heard throughout the room. Foxe wondered if there was some way to indicate he should speak in a more normal tone, but decided to let him go on as he wished. If he was flustered, there was no knowing what he might do.

'Was he not a wealthy man, then?' Foxe dropped his own voice, hoping the alderman might take the hint. Fortunately, his quiet response and attitude of one listening to a confidence seemed to have at least some effect on the other man.

'Wealthy? Yes, I suppose so, in general terms. But all men of business encounter times when trade turns against them. Then they must weather a period of discomfort until their incomes may once again exceed their outgoings.'

'Was Mr. Bonneviot in such a state?'

The rest of the conversation in the coffee house had begin to falter and die away, exactly as they hoped it would. Alderman Halloran was an important man in Norwich and known to be close to the mayor. What he said on this subject would be worth hearing.

'I believe so, Foxe. Fell out with some of his London customers, so he wasn't getting his finished cloth away as quickly as he would do usually. I expect it would all have been sorted out in time, but when he was killed his warehouses were full of unsold cloth and his out-workers and suppliers tired of waiting to receive what he owed them.'

'So a good many will welcome this notice. The lawyer handling Mr. Bonneviot's will, is it?'

'Standard practice, Foxe. Ask any creditors to come forward at once to make their claims. Until they do this, the will can't be proved. The executors won't know exactly what's left for the beneficiaries after all debts have been settled. Of course, if there isn't enough money in total, everyone will get less than they hoped for.'

'Do you think that will be the case, Alderman?' The whole room was virtually silent now.

'To be honest with you, Foxe …' The alderman dropped his voice to a conspiratorial whisper. '… I doubt anyone in this city will get much at all – and that includes the widow and son.'

'How can that be?'

'As I understand it, Bonneviot needed ready money to keep going until he could sort out his quarrel with the Londoners. He was a proud man, you know, so I expect he wanted no one in Norwich to understand the depth of his problem. That's why he went to some London banker for a loan. Got it, of course. No problem there. But then he gets himself murdered.'

'So the loan must be paid back from the estate?'

'Right enough! And you can be sure these London bankers have some clever lawyers to draw up their agreements. The usual pattern in such matters is that the banker gets his money first, then whatever is left goes to the other creditors. The beneficiaries come last.'

'And you think nothing will be left?'

'That's what I've been told. Bonneviot took out a large loan, using his unsold stock as security. Now, that would have been risky, but not unduly so, provided he could sell the stock for a good price over the next few months. Now the bank will seize the stock and sell it all at once for whatever they can get. Sold that way, by auction, when all know the circumstances, I doubt they will raise enough to cover what they lent. That means they'll claim the rest of what they are owed from the remaining estate.'

You could almost feel the excitement in the room now. This was indeed news! Foxe had already seen his friend Sebastian Hirons, the newspaper editor, seated in a quiet corner. How he must be wishing he could hurry off to his office! There was no doubt this information would be spread around Norwich as fast as feet could walk and tongues could wag.

'That's a pretty state of affairs!' Time to change the subject and let the other customers slip away to tell their friends.

'Indeed it is, Foxe. I expect a representative from the bank will be on the next stage from London, brandishing a fistful of legal papers.'

Don't overdo it, Foxe thought to himself. Let them think there may be even more to this story. That way, each will add his own embellishments to supply what he feels has been left unsaid.

'I feel somewhat sorry for the out-workers, sir. They do not receive high wages at the best of times. If they are thrown now into want, they may even cause some disturbance in the city.' Foxe sat back in his chair, trying desperately to signal to the alderman that it was time to move on. Fortunately, the topic of riot and disturbance was well chosen. Alderman Halloran could be depended upon to run after that hare whenever it crossed his path.

'Damned fellows!' he said loudly. 'Always causing some problem or another. Ought to be glad they have work at all! Many who labour on the land are facing far harder times, I dare say. But no, our Norwich men are the most quickly roused of any in the land. The slightest excuse … Well, the mayor will quickly settle their disturbances, if they try it. If the constables can't bring them to order, he'll have the dragoons to them. Blackguards!'

And so he rambled on, while Foxe sat quietly watching one customer ofter another decide it must be time to drink up any remaining coffee and keep some other appointment, forgotten until now. Mr. Hirons hurried off to his newspaper office. Mr. Brandon Seager, editor of the rival Norwich Advertiser, was not far behind him. Others made off in ones and twos until the room seemed nearly empty. Hinman would be bound to hear the news within an hour or so at the most. Now all they could do was trust that the alderman had briefed the lawyer well.

Alderman Halloran seemed to realise on a sudden that the place was nearly empty.

'Good enough, Foxe?' he said.

'Good enough and better, sir. Now, I am sure you have much to do, so I will not keep you. I had best stay a while longer. We have quite ruined the owner's trade for an hour or so, though I daresay it will recover. At least I can make good a little of his loss by ordering more coffee. The matter I spoke to you about – the personal business matter, you understand – is progressing nicely, so we may have occasion to meet in more pleasant circumstances before long.'

It was past the middle of the afternoon when Alfred brought Foxe a note from Alderman Halloran. He found his master in the small room just behind the bookshop. It seemed ages since Foxe had purchased these books from the eighth Earl of Pentelow. The affair of Bonneviot had taken up so much of his time that only now was he able to unpack them and check their condition. Even today, he had found himself unable to concentrate on the task as he should. So much hung in the balance. He had just decided to set them aside again and return to his study, when Alfred came to him.

'The alderman's man said you were to open this note as soon as it was in your hands, sir,' Alfred said. 'He said his master told him it was most urgent.'

Foxe needed no encouragement. Taking the note from Alfred, he broke the seal at once and scanned the contents. Then he sent his man to find young Charlie and tell to run as fast as he could to call Brock to the house.

'Tell him there's a full sixpence for him if Mr. Brock is here within 30 minutes,' Foxe said. 'That should add speed to his legs.'

And, as soon as Alfred left, he read through the alderman's note a second time. In an almost triumphant tone, Alderman Halloran announced that their plan had worked just as they had wished. Mr. James Hinman had called on Mr. Septimus Frewin, the lawyer, at about two o'clock. He had announced his claim, saying he already owned all Bonneviot's unsold stock. To support his claim, he showed Mr. Frewin the bill of sale as evidence. Exactly as they instructed him, the lawyer examined the bill and asked if he might keep it to show it to the executors. He made no comment on its authenticity.

Unfortunately, Hinman refused to allow the bill out of his hands. Mr Frewin showed some presence of mind here, the alderman said. He told Hinman that it was for the executors of Bonneviot's will to decide upon the matter, not him. Until they had accepted the genuineness of Mr. Hinman's claim, they would not release any goods to him. When Hinman still hesitated, he added that he was surprised that the bill was not accompanied by a detailed inventory of the cloth to which it referred. That was the usual practice. Such an inventory was important to ensure that the correct cloth was delivered to the correct purchaser.

This statement had flustered Hinman. The forger would not have been able to produce a convincing inventory. Neither of them had seen the cloth now lying in Bonneviot's warehouse. Yet the lack of such an inventory made the document itself appear suspicious. Hinman had made the best response that he could give. Since the deal was between friends and covered everything in the warehouse, he said, they had not thought an inventory necessary.

Sensing that Hinman was now uncomfortable, Mr. Frewin offered him a way out of the dilemma. He said that he would communicate Hinman's claim to such of the executors as he could contact. He would also ask them to come to his office at noon the next day. Perhaps Mr. Hinman could come at the same time to show the executors the document he possessed. With all the interested parties present, he was sure that they could reach an agreement.

It appeared that Hinman agreed to this suggestion with some relief. The moment he left, Mr. Frewin had sent a message to the alderman telling him what had happened. He had also added that, in his view, the bill of sale was a blatant forgery. No merchant in his thirty years of experience had ever relied upon such a vague document in the matter of a sale of any importance. The absence of a detailed inventory put it beyond doubt. He would be more than willing to testify to that effect before any court in the land.

The alderman now awaited Foxe's word before putting the rest of the plan into action. He had the constables gathered and ready. The sword-bearer and masters-at-arms were at their disposal. Underhill and McSwiggan could be taken as soon as the time was ripe.

Charlie must have flown through the streets, for Brock knocked on the door of the bookshop less than twenty minutes after the boy had set out. Foxe did not waste time going into the details of the alderman's message. He told Brock that Hinman had taken the bait and the trap should now be sprung.

'I will write you a note that you must take to Alderman Halloran's house in Colegate,' Foxe told him. 'Leave the matter of McSwiggan to the constables. If the man is as much of a drunkard as you tell me, it will come as no surprise to any if they seize him and take him to the city goal. He may be taken first, since secrecy is of less consequence there. Underhill, the forger, must be taken as swiftly and silently as possible. Though it is unlikely any word of his arrest could reach Hinman before noon tomorrow, I wish to take no risks. It is likely that Hinman has already found his plan less fool-proof than he thought. He must not be aware that we even suspect who drew up his false document for him.'

'Do you want me and my men to be there?'

'That would be best. I will tell the alderman that the sword-bearer and masters-at-arms should go with you. Stay out of sight until they have secured Underhill. If they fail, take him yourself. If you must do that, be sure to make all legal by handing him over to them at once. Let it be at a time of your choosing, Brock. You and your men best know his habits, and when he may be taken with the least likelihood of arousing suspicion.'

Brock nodded. 'Anything else?'

'Tell the constables to put Underhill somewhere in the gaol where he has no opportunity to make contact with any of the other prisoners. McSwiggan doesn't matter. We will leave them both to reflect on their misdoings overnight. Tomorrow morning we will speak with them … Oh yes, McSwiggan must not be allowed to touch any alcohol. Let him be as desperate for a drink as he can be before we make his acquaintance.'

Brock nodded again. He was never a talkative man, but the tension of this moment seemed to have stilled his tongue completely.

'Wait there, Brock. I will go to my study and write the note for the alderman. I will not be many minutes. I'll send Alfred to you and you can tell him if you would like any refreshment while I am busy.'

'None, thank you.' The sound of his own voice seemed to surprise Brock, for he coughed once or twice and appeared embarrassed at the noise.

Foxe grinned, but said nothing. Like Brock, he would be glad when this matter was concluded. But unlike the older man, all he would be able to do until the morning was wait and fret. Still, there was no point in useless regrets. His part in bringing these rogues to justice lay in the future.

Chapter Sixteen

A Hedge-Attorney

JUST AFTER MIDNIGHT, BROCK SENT WORD THAT HE HAD DONE ALL as Foxe required. The constables had taken McSwiggan late in the afternoon, before he had the opportunity to get drunk. By mid-morning at the latest, his desperation for more alcohol would be extreme. Underhill, the forger, had been called to his door at about ten in the evening. Then they hustled him away into the hands of the sword-bearer and his men before anyone might even notice what was going on. As Foxe had asked, they had lodged him in the gaol and given him no opportunity of speaking with any other person. Foxe could sleep well.

Even so, before he retired Foxe composed a short note to Alderman Halloran and left it for Alfred to deliver early the next morning. In it, he told the alderman that two of the three conspirators were arrested and in custody. It was up to him now to secure the third. Foxe would have liked to supervise the taking of James Hinman in person.

Yet he had come to the conclusion that he should not come face-to-face with the man until he was sure of his ground regarding the other two. They were close to having enough evidence to make a conviction secure, but not quite there. If Underhill and McSwiggan gave evidence for the prosecution, the case against Hinman would be a foregone conclusion.

If only he knew more about Hinman's dealings in Halifax before he came to Norwich. All the information he had was what Hinman had put about himself. He claimed he had worked for one of the principal merchants there. That he had been in charge of his sales of cloth to customers abroad, chiefly in the United Provinces, Denmark and Sweden. Had he been honest in that work? Had he been cheating his master in some way? Most people found a way of acting in the world which suited them and stuck to it. Criminals especially. They became specialists in one type of crime, be it burglary, embezzlement or highway robbery.

Thus Foxe's mind ran around and around, denying him the sleep he craved, until he could bear it no more. Leaving his bed, he put on a warm dressing-gown, lit a candle and went down to his library. There he selected one of his favourite books and settled down to read. Of course, once he did this he fell into a deep sleep almost on the instant.

He was awoken by Alfred, who was not much surprised to find his master asleep in a chair, his book fallen on the floor and the candle burned out. It was often that way when matters were coming to a critical point in one of the adventures he sometimes became involved in. He retrieved the book, woke Foxe as gently as he might and waited while his master stretched and groaned himself into full consciousness.

'What's the time, Alfred?'

'A little before eight o'clock, sir. If you would like to return to your room, I will have the maid bring you a jug of hot water there, so that you may wash and let me shave you. Would you like Mrs. Dobbins to serve your breakfast earlier than usual, since you are awake?'

Foxe indicated that he would and stumbled up the stairs to his room. Half way up, he turned and enquired whether Alfred had delivered his note to the alderman's house.

'I had just returned from taking it there myself when I found you, sir,' Alfred told him. 'Alderman Halloran's footman said his master had not yet arisen, but he would be sure to place it into his hands the instant he did.'

'Thank you, Alfred. Please send the boy to call Mr. Brock to wait on me immediately after I have eaten.'

'Mr. Brock is already here, sir. I suspect he too found it hard to sleep, for he looks as if he has not laid eyes on his bed for many hours. Mrs. Dobbins laid a place for him at the kitchen table. I gather he has already consumed half a dozen eggs and three fresh rolls and is drinking the house dry of chocolate. I trust that we have acted as you would wish?'

'As always, Alfred. Let Brock finish his breakfast in peace. Bring me two rolls with butter and jam. Also a little cheese. Chocolate too, of course, if our guest has left me some. I will eat in my room.'

As Alfred nodded and moved away, Foxe mused on the day before them. Underhill first, he said to himself. If Brock is looking even more of a villain than usual, that will be to our advantage. He was sure Hinman must have obtained money from somewhere to set himself up as the kind of person Bonneviot would listen to. Even if it had been his plan from the start to cheat the man, did he also intend murder? The hiring of McSwiggan to kill Bonneviot had many of the marks of a hasty response, concocted under the pressure of strong emotion. For all the rest, Hinman's planning had been careful and precise. He had failed in the matter of an inventory to go with his fake bill of sale, of course. Yet that might have been no more than the unfamiliarity of someone unused to those kinds of transactions. It might even have come about for no better reason that the plain fact that he had no precise idea of what cloth was in the warehouse. He could not have gone there to make note of what he was planning to steal.

How to present himself to Underhill? Not as Foxe, that was sure. He needed an alias who had a direct interest in the forgery itself as a means of making sure Hinman went to the gallows. Yet it must also be someone without much in the way of scruples in achieving his desire. Underhill must believe any threats they made were serious.

Thus Foxe reasoned with himself as he washed his face and Alfred shaved him. In the end, he thought he had found the perfect answer. Pulling clothes from cupboards and boxes – Alfred would put all away later – he found what he needed. A dark frock-coat a year or more out of fashion and a waistcoat that he had regretted purchasing the moment it was delivered. He added plain worsted breeches and blue woollen stockings. The final touch was an old pair of shoes whose quality was well below his normal standards. Then he topped off all with a wig and hat of similar shabby appearance. Now, he thought, he would look the part of Mr. Hamilton Foxearth, one of the many second- and third-rate lawyers who infested the city. These men spent their lives pursuing vexatious litigation for clients without the means to pay someone better trained. None, in his experience, were honest. Mr. Foxearth would claim to be speaking on behalf of one of the smaller merchants Bonneviot's death must have left with unpaid debts. A dealer in linen yarn from Ireland might seem most credible. Brock could attend as his clerk. Though they claimed to be men of the law, such vermin as Mr. Foxearth often backed up legal arguments with more direct means of persuasion.

Thus, having eaten his breakfast and dressed himself in this regrettable manner, Foxe went down to the kitchen to collect Brock. A pretty pair they made indeed. Mr. Foxearth was the image of a man more ready to twist and pervert the laws of the land than see them enforced. His clerk, Brock, could only have been a clerk in name. His unwashed face, thick with stubble, and his bloodshot eyes suggested he would be more able with his fists than a pen.

'No, Brock. You must not wash, nor make yourself look less of a rogue. You are perfect as you are. Here, cram this dreadful hat on your head and try to slouch a little more. Excellent! I have already asked the alderman to inform the gaoler that Joshua Underhill will have two visitors this morning. When they give the password 'haywain', they are to be admitted without further question. Quickly now. We must do all before noon, if we can, and that includes time for you to visit McSwiggan on your own.'

'Before we leave, wouldn't it be best to tell me who the devil you are pretending to be and what we are going to do?'

'Don't you recognise Mr. Hamilton Foxearth, the eminent lawyer?'

'Eminent fraudster, you mean. Eminent hedge-attorney. By God, one look at him and you know his case and his evidence are a mass of perjury and falsehood.'

'Precisely, Brock. Now, if such a one came with a mixture of smoothly told lies and poorly concealed threats, would you be surprised?'

'What do you take me for? That kind of man deals in nothing else!'

'And what would his clerk be?'

'Some ruffian without learning or scruples. Someone ready to turn his employers threats into blows and his property claims into arson, if they were not met.'

'There, Brock. You knew your role all along. Now, let us waste no more time. We will leave by the gate from the garden. Alfred, scout ahead and let us know when none are around. I would not wish them to see what guests that most respectable bookseller, Mr. Ashmole Foxe, has been harbouring in his house. Then it is all speed for the gaol to give our cunning forger a taste of his own medicine.'

❧

They found Mr. Joshua Underhill possessed of a mighty rage of righteous anger at his treatment the night before. Not knowing they had any part in his arrest, he launched at once into a series of complaints and accusations.

Mr. Foxearth listened intently. Sometimes he injected a supportive comment. Sometimes he turned to his clerk and cried out incomprehensible phases. 'There is a visio doctrinae falsae if ever I saw one!' he said at one point. Later he shouted 'Habeas corpus mutabilis must be claimed at once!' And at the end, 'Secundum ordinem Melchisidek I say to that.'

At length, Mr. Underhill paused for breath. Mr. Foxearth had established at the start that Underhill had no one to represent him, nor any means of paying someone if he had. At once he offered his services – pro bono nunquam, of course – and poured scorn on the actions of the authorities in treating an honest man thus.

'Have they told you why you were taken in this barbarian way, sir? Have they?'

'They charged me with forging a document – a bill of sale, I believe.'

'Which, of course, you would never do!'

'Never!'

'What is your profession, sir, if I may ask?'

'I am a scrivener.'

'A scrivener! So your work itself is to write legal documents, is it not? Are they charging you with the crime of following your profession? Even if you had written such a document – which you vehemently deny – it would be no crime. It is the way you earn an honest living. But tell me, just between ourselves, did you write such a document? You see, if you admitted to doing so, it would make your defence yet stronger. To write such a document is no offence at all, neither by statute nor by common law. Yet to use it fraudulently – say with a certain signature added – would be to utter a forgery. That is punishable by death.'

'Death?' Underhill's voice was barely a squeak.

'In every case. No reprieve or mitigation allowed. Indeed, the law holds it to be a form of treason. Thus it is punishable by hanging, drawing and quartering.' That punishment had fallen into disuse long ago, but Foxe suspected Underhill would not know it.

'Hanging, drawing and ...'

'Quartering, sir. Partly hanged, cut down, castrated, disembowelled alive and then ...'

'C...c...castrated...?' Underhill looked as if he was going to be sick.

'Fear not, dear sir. You may trust in Hamilton Foxearth. I know exactly how to remove this terrible threat from your person. Only help me a little and I will make sure you you face no worse a charge than aiding and abetting.'

'Help you?'

Underhill's natural suspicions were aroused, despite his terror at the thought of facing the ancient punishment for high treason.

'It is but a small thing, sir. My concern in this matter is not with you, but with the man who commissioned you.'

'Commissioned me?'

'But of course. He is the criminal. He it is who should be facing the gallows, not you. He has used the document you wrote in all innocence ... you did write it, I take it?' Underhill nodded agreement. 'You wrote the document innocently. It is he who has used it to perpetrate a most abominable fraud against my client, a respectable yarn merchant. He has claimed to own goods – using the document you wrote and based on the signature you added for him …' Underhill nodded again. '… to cheat my other client out of a significant sum of money owed to him by one Master Bonneviot, once a merchant of this city. If I can prove this document to be false, based on your sworn evidence …'

Underhill suddenly realised that he was being asked to give evidence in court that he had forged a document being used to cheat people out of money. At once, he began to protest. He had done nothing of the kind. No one had ever commissioned him in that way. He was completely innocent of ever having set eyes on Mr. Hinman.

Since that man's name had not yet been mentioned, Underhill had just proved his guilt beyond doubt. He had also named his co-conspirator in the presence of two witnesses.

'Oh dear, Brock. I fear Mr. Underhill is going to prove difficult. And it was such a small favour in return for freeing him from almost certain death. Maybe you can persuade him of the mistake he is making?'

Brock moved forward to tower over Underhill, forcing the man back until he was pressed up against the wall.

'Listen, cully!' he growled. 'Mr. Foxearth may be a mild and patient man, but I ain't. What 'e's telling you is plain good sense. You may be a fool, but that Hinman ain't. If 'e's brought before a judge, you be damn sure 'e'll lay all the blame on you. Say you gave him the document and told him it was genuine. Now, since 'e's gentry and you're scum, who d'you think the jury will believe? You'll be for the drop and he'll walk off smiling.'

Underhill was shaking now. 'But he said if I ever told anyone …'

'He ain't here and I am. Do what the nice Mr. Foxearth says, turn King's Evidence, and you'll save your scrawny neck. That Hinman can't save you, even if 'e wanted to – which I'm certain 'e don't.'

'But if I deny everything, and he does too, they'll be no case.'

'D'you think they'd go to court with nothing better than a snivelling forger and a fake gentleman? They'll have plenty of other evidence, believe me. Besides, suppose 'e did act like that and you was let off. D'you know what would happen then?'

Underhill stayed silent, his eyes staring into Brock's face, now no more than an inch or two from his own.

'You says you're a scrivener. Right?'

'I am.'

'A man what makes his bread by writing things. Now, suppose such a one was to meet with a nasty accident. Say 'e happened to break both his hands, so that 'e couldn't hold a pen, let alone write. What use is a forger who can't forge? Tell me that, cully!'

'I'll do it! I swear! Just leave me alone!'

'Now 'e's seeing sense,' Brock said to Foxe.

'I knew he would,' Foxe replied. 'Brock, give me the pen and paper and we'll take his deposition right away, then he can swear to it before Alderman Halloran, who should be waiting somewhere near.'

It took little enough time after that. Underhill stated that Hinman had approached him and asked him to write out a bill of sale for Bonneviot's stock of cloth. Simply that. Only when it was done did he demand that it be dated exactly three weeks earlier. Then he produced a paper bearing a man's signature and told Underhill to add the signature to the document. That final demand he accompanied with both threats and a suitable reward, with the promise of more to come.

Foxe wrote it all down, omitting Underhill's constant attempts to excuse his own conduct, read it back to him and told the man to sign it. This he did, conscious of the sound of Brock cracking his knuckles just behind him. When that was done, Foxe called the alderman and they added their own, genuine signatures. Now, if the man tried to go back on his words, he would face a charge of perjury to go along with the rest.

That was Underhill settled. Now they must move to the others. The alderman left at once to proceed to Mr. Septimus Frewin's place of business, where Hinman was due at noon. When he arrived, the executors would ask to inspect his bill of sale. Once that was in their hands, the signal would be given and James Hinman arrested for forgery and murder.

Brock left to deal with McSwiggan. There seemed little danger that he would fail to name Hinman as the one who had hired him to commit murder. If he remained silent, he would hang. If he spoke out, he would at least save his life and be transported to the American colonies. Most likely he would die there of drink or disease. He would not be mourned.

As for Foxe, once again he must go home and wait for news. He had done too much of that recently. It was making him bad-tempered. As he left, he told himself that interviewing Hinman would at last allow him to work off some of those choleric feelings. The man had caused him a great deal of trouble. Now it was his turn.

Chapter Seventeen

The Quarry is Lost

BROCK CAME WITHIN THE HOUR. As he predicted, McSwiggan had given in quickly. Was it the hope of evading the noose or the sight of a flask of gin in Brock's hand which most affected his decision? It scarcely mattered. He had said clearly that it was Hinman who paid him to murder Bonneviot. Even told him exactly when and where he might find him in the ideal spot. Brock had written it all down as his statement, persuaded the man to add a shaky cross at the bottom and called the gaoler to add his witness to Brock's own.

Now both men waited. Noon came and passed. One o'clock came and passed also without word from the alderman. It was past half-past one when they heard a great banging on the door of the bookshop and Alfred hastened to answer it.

A moment or so later, Alderman Halloran himself burst into the room. His wig was askew on his head, his hat still in his hand and even the buttons on his coat done up askew. Yet what was worst of all, his face was so red and his breathing so rapid and laboured that he must have done the unthinkable for such a dignified man – hastened to Foxe's house on foot!

He wasted no time on any greeting or preamble. The moment he was capable of speech, he cried out, 'He did not come! Hinman did not come! We waited an hour past the appointed time without result. He sent no message either. He has flown, damn it! We've lost him!'

'Sit and calm yourself, sir,' Foxe said. He turned to speak to Brock but saw he was already making his way to the door. 'Tell me what took place.'

'Nothing took place! The man never put in an appearance!'

'No message either?'

'None. He has escaped us, Foxe, God's curse upon him for the worst of villains! The mayor and I had set our hearts on having him in the dock at the next assizes. Now he is gone.'

'Well, we will know soon enough,' Foxe said. 'I had set a watch upon him. If he left the inn where he was staying, they had orders to follow close behind. If he tried to leave the city, they were to stop him. Brock has gone already to find out what they can tell us. Hinman will not get far. I am sure of that. What puzzles me is how he got wind of our having found him out.'

'It was that fool lawyer, if you ask me, questioning him about inventories and the like. The man must have realised his forgery would not be accepted and run right away.'

'You may be right, Alderman. Yet he had come so far and was so close to attaining his goal … Would he give up without at least one further effort? He had almost a day to dream up some plausible excuse for the lack of the extra document. I had not placed him as a man lacking daring or resolution.'

'Let us hope your man Brock can find him again. It would stick in my gullet to have him escape us, after all the trouble he has caused.'

'And mine also. Now, sir, take your ease for a moment and regain your composure. Brock will not return for a good while, I expect. In the meantime, when you are ready you may go back to your house and become – at least indirectly – the bearer of good news instead of bad. There is no need for further delay in settling Bonneviot's affairs. Let word be sent to Master Burford to pay all the outstanding debts and wages, as soon as he has sufficient funds in his hands. Concealment of what you have arranged will bring no more benefit. We may allow the world to see that the powerful men of this city are awake and alive to deal with any threats to its prosperity.'

As Foxe suspected, such stirring words put some vigour back into the alderman. He and the mayor liked nothing so much as the opportunity to win the approval of the citizens of Norwich for some heroic action. Elections were not far off. To be able to claim they had saved the city from ruin would give them the topic for many a rousing speech on the hustings. Of course, all knew the number of votes received came directly from the size of the bribes paid to the voters. Still, it was good to have some means of concealing that fact behind a screen of grandiose oratory.

'You're right, Foxe. No need for poor men to remain in want without reason. I suppose I must also report to the mayor, though I take little pleasure in the prospect. He will be much vexed, I dare say.'

'I am sure you will be able to calm him, Alderman. Let him reflect more on the fact that you have saved the major manufacture of this city from great harm. Even if Hinman escapes, that fact is sure. We also have Bonneviot's murderer under arrest, together with a notorious forger, who might yet have caused loss to many a merchant and business owner.'

'True, true enough, Foxe. The mayor is a vain man …' Just as you are, Foxe thought to himself. '… and loves nothing better than to be able to claim he has done some mighty deed. Send word to me of what Brock has discovered, won't you?'

Brock returned more quickly than Foxe had predicted, but his grim expression proved he did not bring good news. 'Our bird has flown,' he said. 'Last night. Two men came to the inn and went up to his room. A little later, 'e came down with them and left by the rear door.'

'How did your watcher there miss him?' Foxe did not insult Brock's intelligence by asking if he had taken such an elementary precaution.

Brock let out a sharp, mirthless laugh. 'By one of the oldest tricks in the book. The man was growing bored after so many days seeing nothing. When a pair o' young whores came up and started to ply him with sweet words, kisses and caresses, 'e let them draw him into the shadows. He swears it was only for a moment, but I dare say it took him longer than that to 'ave 'is pleasure of one or both o' them. 'E'll not work for me again.'

'Do not be too hard on him, Brock. Indeed, the fault is mine almost as much as his. I was sure Hinman was working on his own in this affair. This is the first time we have come across anyone aiding him. I had never considered such a possibility, fool that I am.'

'Will you come to the inn with me? You may be able to get more from the innkeeper than I have. Something – or someone – has 'im frightened.'

They left at once and headed first along Pottergate, then turned left and went a little way up the road that led towards Cromer. At The Royal George Inn, a well-kept and substantial building set back a little from the road, Brock led the way inside. Foxe had decided to stay in his gentleman's clothing. The politeness and helpfulness of innkeepers, in his experience, rose or fell according to their hopes of future profit.

Joseph Eason, the innkeeper, proved to be typical of the breed: brawny from handling barrels and red-faced from checking the quality of their contents. Spotting Foxe, he was at once full of oily subservience.

'Mr. Hinman, sir? A friend of yours, was 'e?'

'No,' Foxe replied shortly. 'Say more a man who was due to come to me this morning to settle a large debt.'

As he hoped, this loosened the innkeeper's tongue. He need not defend anyone who had done harm to such a fine gentlemen as now stood before him.

'I knew 'e was not to be trusted, sir. That's why I made 'im pay each week in advance.'

As you do all your guests, I warrant, Foxe thought, for you are as greedy a bastard as I have seen in many a year.

'Odd 'e was too,' the innkeeper said

'How was he odd?'

'He'd go out after 'e'd breakfasted, looking smart, and return only in time for dinner. Then 'e stayed in his room. Took all 'is meals there too. Never 'ad any visitors till last night.'

'He remained alone?'

'Yes. Regular hermit. Didn't bother the girls who took up 'is food neither. Not that one or two would have minded. He was a youngish man, that Mr. Hinman, and not bad looking. I don't keep a disorderly house, you understand …' But I wager you take a large cut of what your girls earn by their unofficial whoring, Foxe thought. '… but, well, some of those who lodges 'ere are far from home and lonely. If a girl wishes to comfort 'em for a while …' As you have instructed her doubtless. '… I am not one to interfere.'

'No whores, then.'

'Oh no, sir. Nor boys either. Once or twice none of our waitresses was free to take up Mr. Hinman's meal. Then I 'ad to send a kitchen lad instead.' More comforters, I dare say, Foxe said inside his head. If you can't make money by prostituting your female servants, you try with a pretty kitchen boy. What a miserable wretch you are, man!

'No one at all.'

'Not until the two men what came last night and asked which room Mr. Hinman was staying in. I 'ad no reason not to tell them now, did I sir? No reason at all. Though I was surprised that such a man as Mr. Hinman should know two of Jack Beeston's men.'

Foxe felt Brock's sharp intake of breath as much as heard it. He must know the name.

'How long were they upstairs? Did you notice?' I'll bet you did, Foxe thought. You sensed trouble.

'Perhaps ten minutes? No more.'

'And the three left together? Did they seem on good terms?'

'Well, that was odd …' The innkeeper caught himself in time. 'Yes indeed, sir. Mr. Hinman walked with them as calm as you like.'

'He was not being forced in any way.'

'Certainly not! If I had thought that …' You would have looked the other way, Foxe supplied.

'Well, it seems I have missed him. He may have left a note for me though. Will you show me the room he lodged in? No need to trouble yourself to come up. Just tell us which it was.'

The innkeeper would, though it took the persuasive power of half a guinea to keep him safely below.

The room looked as if Hinman had stepped out for a moment and would soon return. Two excellent suits of clothes hung in a cupboard. One good pair of shoes were beneath them. Two good shirts and two pairs of well-made breeches. Two pairs of silk stockings. It seemed

Hinman had two of everything. He was probably wearing the other pair of good shoes when he left.

But what else had he been wearing? As they looked around, they found his other clothes – and there were few enough – were of far poorer quality. A stained and dirty night-shirt lay on the bed. A clothes-box contained a single pair of cheap woollen stockings. A shirt was found that had been patched and turned more than once. A pair of much-used linen breeches and a single handkerchief of threadbare calico. On a small cupboard by the bed was a fine wig on a stand and a box of wig-powder, about half used. No hat or overcoat. No money, though that did not signify much. If Hinman had been absent all night, and in doubtful company, it would not have taken the noble innkeeper long to play the part of opportunist thief.

They took a few more moments for Brock to feel under the bed and check for any obvious hiding places. Then they concluded there was nothing more to be learned either in the room itself or in the inn.

#

Once they were outside, Foxe asked Brock about Jack Beeston. The name had meant something to him, though Foxe could not recall hearing of the man before.

'I dare say you wouldn't have,' Brock said. 'You don't move in 'is circles.'

'What circles?'

'Pimps, standover men, bawds, pickpockets, petty thieves, beggars. All the worst scum o' this fair city.'

'No, I do not, I'm glad to say. Now, back to Jack Beeston.'

'He's a man of the worst sort. Owns a string of filthy whorehouses, as well as grog-shops and gambling dens. Makes the small shopkeepers pay him, unless they want 'is men to ruin their goods and wreck their premises. Thieves sell 'im what they've stolen and gets ready cash, though 'e gives them as little as 'e can.'

'Why not go elsewhere?'

'Do that and his ruffians will break your legs! He's also a moneylender. Charges huge amounts of interest. Extorts payment by threats and beatings.'

'He sounds delightful. So that was where Hinman got the money he needed.'

'Surely not! I doubt an outsider would even know 'e existed, especially if 'e was a person of the middling sort.'

'No, Brock. He's our man, I'm sure of it. Hinman needed a good amount of money and quickly. He couldn't go to the regular bankers. He was supposed to be a person of some prosperity. A successful businessman from Halifax. He had to find someone who would lend in secret and ask few questions.'

'Jack Beeston would do that, but you'd be in a tight spot if you couldn't pay when the time came.'

'As Hinman was shortly to be. He should have been pleading with us to lock him up before his moneylender friend could come and find him.'

'Yes, I suppose that makes sense. Beeston discovered, or sensed, Hinman might not be able to pay what 'e owed and got to 'im before we could.'

'I imagine Beeston was either watching Hinman, as we were, or discovered he had been to the forger and was up to something shady. Would Hinman even have let Beeston in on the plot, do you think?'

'Not if he had any sense! Beeston would agree, right enough. Then 'e'd want a good share of the proceeds and would extort more from Hinman afterwards in return for keeping 'is mouth shut.'

'Might Underhill, the forger, have been known to Beeston?'

'Of course! Probably on his payroll. That explains Beeston's suspicions now. So long as 'e thought Hinman 'ad a chance of succeeding, 'e'd stay silent. Then, afterwards, 'e'd turn up and demand payment for keeping mum, as I said. But once Underhill was taken …'

'Beeston would have guessed the authorities had caught on to the plot.'

'He would indeed!'

'So, we know who has Hinman and why.'

'And what his chances are!'

'Quite so, but what else did our visit to Hinman's room tell us?'

'That 'e was not what 'e said 'e was. Sure, 'e had enough good clothes to wear out to impress people, but not so long ago 'e'd been in a much less wealthy state.'

'Exactly. Now, I have already asked the mayor to find out all he can about Hinman's past dealings in Halifax. My guess is that we will find he was a poor clerk in some master-weaver's employ. Or he had once held a higher position, but was dismissed for theft or embezzlement. He knew enough about the cloth trade to sound good and fool Bonneviot, but he was clearly not what he claimed to be.'

'What do we do now, Foxe?'

'We go home and get some rest. I am tired out by all today's surprises, as you must be. No, don't argue. Go home and rest. Tomorrow we will have much to do. We are not beaten yet, Brock. You must find out all you can about where Beeston might have taken Hinman and what he is doing with him. I will report to the alderman and tell him what further action I propose.'

'Which is?'

'I have no idea yet! Hopefully, rest, food and a quiet evening will bring me inspiration. If not …'

'You'll spend the rest of the day with one of the Catt sisters.'

'What an excellent idea, Brock. Why didn't I think of it? I believe it's Kitty's turn …'

'They'll ruin your health! Even one would try the stamina of any man, as I hear. But both on 'em …'

'Go home, Brock! Now, I say! Go home!'

Chapter Eighteen

Multiple Pursuits

DESPITE BROCK'S SUGGESTION, FOXE DID not GO TO SEE either of the Catt sisters that day or the next. He had intended to do so, but what he learned when he called on Alderman Halloran drove all else from his mind.

Foxe found the alderman in a state of high excitement. He obviously had some news he was on tenterhooks to pass on. Yet first he asked Foxe to relate what he had discovered about Hinman's disappearance. That was the most pressing issue, he said.

Foxe explained what Brock and he had discovered. How Hinman had received two visitors, who had escorted him from the inn where he had been staying. He revealed the simple trick they had played to get the man away unnoticed by Brock's watcher. Finally, he told the alderman who these men were and what he guessed about the purpose of their visit.

'So Hinman is in the hands of this villain, Beeston. We shall probably never see him again, unless we find his body in a ditch somewhere.'

'That may well be the outcome, Alderman. Yet what bothers me is why Beeston decided to seize the man now. By doing so, he ensured Hinman's whole scheme was ruined. He would be unable to pay back whatever he owed. He must have thought he already knew what the outcome must be, so had nothing to lose by bringing all to an end. And how he discovered that, I have no inkling.'

'No. Yet it must be the case. Now, I can be no help with that matter. Yet what I have learned only this morning may explain enough. I believe I know the reason for Hinman going to Beeston for money in the first place. And why he would have run anyway, the minute he learned we were enquiring about him.'

So, Foxe was right. The alderman did have news. Yet he sensed also that what he had revealed about Hinman's involvement with Beeston had in some way spilled a little of the wind from the alderman's sails.

'I had a message from the mayor this morning, asking me to call on him at once. I don't mind telling you that I arrived feeling quite apprehensive. I feared he had considered all I told him yesterday and especially that Hinman was flown. His surprise was so great at the time that he had said little. Now I imagined he realised what it all meant and would upbraid me severely for the loss.'

'But it was not your fault!'

'Such things as logic and consideration do not weigh on our worthy mayor's mind at the best of times.'

'Yes, I have heard he is not a tolerant man when things do not go his way.'

'Imagine my surprise when he ignored my attempts to start on my defence and said that he had already decided I was not at fault.'

Foxe looked suitably surprised, though he judged the mayor might seem to forgive, but would recall the matter any time when he felt he needed to bring the alderman to order.

'What he wished to tell me,' the alderman continued, 'was that he had received a response to his enquiry about Mr. James Hinman from the Mayor of Halifax. It seems none in that town have ever heard the name! There neither is, nor was, a person employed by any master-weaver thereabouts who was called James Hinman. No, not from the most trusted factotum to the humblest out-worker. The Mayor of Halifax had even made enquiries in Bradford. In case, he wrote – and this angered our mayor – we had confused what he called 'the two premier manufacturing towns for woollens in the kingdom'.

'I can well imagine such effrontery would not have been pleasing to His Worship,' Foxe said.

'Indeed it was not! I had some trouble in dissuading him from sending a most insulting reply. In the end, he agreed that remarks of that kind should be ignored, thus indicating a suitable contempt for both the content and the occasion.'

'Hinman not known there! I can scarce even begin to understand what this may mean. Did he come from some other centre of the making of worsted cloth? Paisley, perhaps, or even the area in the Cotswold Hills where men are now establishing factories? He must have obtained a good knowledge of the business from somewhere. Without that, he could not convince Bonneviot it would be worth making a deal with him.'

'Indeed. Bonneviot was not a man to be fooled easily. However much he was in need of money and an outlet for his unsold stocks, he would never have taken any man on trust, let alone one from outside the city.'

'Maybe Hinman came from London and had worked for one of the merchants there?'

'Maybe. All in London associated with our business already knew of Bonneviot's quarrel and the merchants' response. Yet if Hinman came from London, why did he not simply suggest that Bonneviot could deal with him there? That he would take the place of those Bonneviot had quarrelled with? Why include all the extra complexity of dealings overseas?'

'I'm sorry, Alderman. My mind is so confused with possibilities to account for this news that I can scarce grasp anything of what it may mean. It is even leading me to ask if there ever was a deal agreed with Bonneviot. Perhaps they had discussed such a deal – even agreed it in principle – then Bonneviot was killed and all seemed lost. That might account for Hinman's subsequent actions. I have always thought these based more on improvisation that careful strategy.'

'But there was a deal. We know there was.'

'It's no use, Alderman. I need time to think more. It seems to me that much of what we have believed we knew until now must be flawed in some way. We have perforce made many assumptions to cover gaps in our knowledge. I fear one or more of those will prove to have pointed us along the wrong path. All I can do is to work through everything again from the beginning, hoping to spot the place where I went wrong.'

'Well, there is little need for haste now, Foxe. Let the processes of justice deal with the forger and the assassin. We have their confessions. No need in present circumstances for either to turn King's Evidence. I will have them brought before me this afternoon and commit both to the next convenient assizes. At least they will trouble us no more.'

Foxe sat silent for so long that Alderman Halloran had to clear his throat twice, and loudly, to gain his attention and indicate he should leave. Yet when the bookseller finally emerged from his reverie, it was with a sudden access of energy quite out of place compared with what had gone before.

'A thought has come to me that warrants further enquiry, sir, and that urgently. I would be most grateful if you would ask amongst all the master weavers of the city to discover which of them Hinman had approached before settling on Bonneviot.'

'I imagine many of them, Foxe. Why should it matter now?'

'It is of great importance I believe. You should also ask what story he told each. Was it the same as he told Bonneviot, so far as we know? Did he refine it as he went along? Was it by speaking with such men that he picked up enough seeming knowledge to dress his words to Bonneviot in suitable garb?'

'Very well, Foxe, I will do as you ask. Though for the life of me I cannot see what you are driving at.'

'It is not quite clear to me either, Alderman. I am proceeding by instinct, not sure knowledge. Something tells me that we will discover Hinman refining his approach. The extent of his knowledge of which master weavers to contact first may also show the source of his knowledge about our city and its industry. At the least, it is worth trying, for I cannot see where else we can make progress.'

Brock came just as Foxe was preparing to go in to dine, so Foxe immediately invited him to the table. No, he said, he would not stay to eat. Foxe was sad to see his friend look so careworn. Brock had taken the escape of Hinman as a personal failure on his part. Nothing Foxe could say would change that. Somehow, Brock must be left to work out his own way of forgiving himself, probably through constant work until the man could be found again.

'Very well, Brock,' Foxe said to him. 'I know you will not rest until you have that rogue back under your hand. Yet I tell you again that no one – myself least of all – holds you responsible for his escape. You did everything I asked of you. If there is any blame, it is mine for failing to recognise a possible danger.'

Brock ignored this and launched at once into his own news. 'We aren't the only ones seeking Hinman. By God, he's a slippery cove! It seems he gave Beeston's men the slip and ran off. Now Jack Beeston 'as 'is own resources out in force. He's put the word out amongst all the thieves, footpads, pickpockets, whores and layabouts in Norwich. He'll give a fine reward to whoever can bring 'im news that lets this man be taken. Of course, being the wretch 'e is, 'e's also added the promise of harsh treatment indeed for any foolish enough to aid Hinman in 'is escape. It's a rare mess.'

'So … Hinman ran away. Amazing! I wonder how he managed that? If Beeston finds him before we do …'

'Which 'e probably will. He 'as twice the searchers we have and contacts amongst all the worst elements in the city and beyond. We've lost 'im for good, as I see it. Damn the man!'

'Well if Beeston finds Hinman first, so be it. Cheer up, Brock. I know it would be good to discover the truth about this affair. Still, I doubt Hinman would be willing to confess to us. In the end, Providence will determine all. But listen. I spoke earlier to the alderman. He brought the most surprising news from the mayor.'

Foxe told Brock all he had learned, how Hinman was not who or what he claimed to be, and how they must have been on the wrong path all along.

'What do you make of that, Brock?' Foxe said at the end.

'It goes from bad to worse! It makes my 'ead ache! Why did you 'ave to tell me all that when we've probably no chance of ever discovering the truth? Now I don't even know who I let get away.'

'Come, old friend. Don't be so downhearted. Sit, eat and help me work out what this may mean. They say two heads are better than one, and yours is the head I would always choose to help me. You can do no more useful task than this. It will serve us far better than running around the city, half a step behind Beeston's ruffians.'

Slowly, Brock let himself be persuaded. Mrs. Dobbins produced enough food for two and more besides – from where, Foxe did not ask – and the two men set to with healthy appetites.

At length, relaxing over a glass or two of fine port, Foxe returned to the problem of Hinman's actions.

'When I spoke about it before, Brock, you said you did not believe Hinman would have been foolish enough to let Beeston in on the plot. He must have concocted a different story to support his need for money. Either that or used the tale he told everyone else about being a wealthy man temporarily in need of extra funds. Which?'

'The second. Why dream up another story when you 'as one as is already shown to work? Besides, Beeston keeps 'is eyes and ears open for all that goes on in this city, in case it should offer him profit. If Hinman had produced a different tale from what 'e told others, Beeston would've been mighty suspicious.'

'I agree. So Hinman uses the same tale, adding something to account for a temporary shortage of case. Perhaps he claimed to be awaiting some payment due to him, or the collection of a large debt. Something like that. Would Beeston have been taken in?'

'That depends on the source of the money to come. He would never accept the idea of someone of the middling sort approaching 'im for money. Not unless the reason for their need was something disreputable. If it was a simple delay in payment of a legitimate debt, why not borrow from a friend or business associate?'

'Because Hinman was far from home in a strange city?'

'No, no. That wouldn't do. He could use a servant or a trusted agent to get the money for 'im where 'e was known and trusted. No, it would have to be money from some action 'e did not wish to become known. Perhaps he claimed to be owed some money by a lonely wife to hush up an affair between them. No … he doesn't seem to like women. Suppose he had been involved with the perverted son of a wealthy father. Maybe he enjoyed the boy's favours, or sent him to someone else who would, then turned to blackmail. The boy dare not ask 'is father for the money outright, but claims he can find the cash elsewhere. Meanwhile Hinman holds the threat over 'is head of telling the father his lad is a sodomite if 'e does not. Something like that.'

'Yes, that makes sense. So, on that basis, Hinman has been indulging in something he certainly does not wish his fine business friends to know about. Sodomy, adultery, pimping or something even worse. He tells Beeston he was relying on the money to finance some other matter, but now has to wait for payment. So why does Beeston suddenly send his standover men to demand his money back?'

'He thinks 'e's going to lose it. Can't see why else.'

'Indeed. But why now? Let's think it through. Suppose Beeston learns that Hinman has consulted a forger to produce a fake document. Would that be enough?'

'No. Not as I see it. Beeston is the foulest of criminals, evil through and through. If Hinman also proves to be dishonest in some way, that wouldn't make 'im any less of a source of profit. More, perhaps. Beeston would ask Underhill the nature of the document. When 'e learned it wasn't anything to do with, say, a gambling debt, 'e would've smelled profitable villainy and tried to take advantage of it.'

'Again, you are right, I'm sure. What about when – or if – Beeston learns Underhill has been arrested?'

'That would give 'im some cause for worry, right enough. Even so, Underhill was an habitual forger. It was 'is business, under all that nonsense of being a scrivener. There'd be nothing to say 'is arrest had anything to do with 'is dealings with Hinman.'

'Right yet again! Now, if I were Beeston, what would I do? I think I might take note that someone – but not someone in league with the law, so far as Beeston knows – is watching Hinman, just as he is. Maybe Hinman has borrowed money elsewhere. Maybe the forged document from Underhill was to do with that matter. I would wish to know, that's certain. If Hinman is running a number of tricks of that nature, I – as Beeston – would want to be able to take profit from them all.'

'You have the man down perfectly, Foxe. Devious, cunning, without any scruple and always on the watch for a chance to make yet more geld. I hate the bastard!'

'So … yes, I have it … I send my men to slip Hinman away from the other watchers and bring him to me, so that I may find out what he is up to. They do not seize him physically, so long as he is willing to come of his own accord. Beeston is not unduly anxious, merely curious.'

'Then Hinman on a sudden stops being co-operative and gets away from 'is escort. They aren't expecting that and 'e's off before they can grab at 'im. Maybe darts into some alley, or manages to find a spot to hide and let 'em pass.'

'Now Beeston is both anxious and angry to boot. If Hinman was telling him the truth when he lent the money, he would have no reason to run off. He could not know that Beeston had discovered his other scheme with Underhill. The fact that he ran …'

'Must mean that Beeston 'as been gulled!' Brock cried. 'That's it! Got to be! Beeston's always ready to cheat others, but to be cheated 'isself …! That above all would rouse him to fury. Oh, I wish I could've seen 'im when 'is men reported Hinman 'ad slipped from them. He would've foamed at the mouth like the mad dog 'e is! Nor, I reckon, would he've been as forgiving of their mistake as you have been of mine.'

'You made no mistake, Brock. How many more times do I have to tell you? But you are right about such a loathsome toad as Beeston. I imagine he indeed took out his anger on those men, before proclaiming that Hinman must be found and brought to him alive. Even now, I imagine, he is taking pleasure in considering the fate he has in mind for Hinman when he is taken.'

'Then Hinman should pray to God that 'e either escapes or dies in the attempt. His fate at Beeston's hands doesn't bear thinking about.'

'Then we will not do so, Brock. Now, as I predicted, you have helped me solve the matter of Beeston and Hinman. At least, so far as it may be solved until we know whether Hinman has got away. That is enough for today. Let us enjoy this fine wine and talk of lighter matters. Then you must go home and take your rest. Tomorrow I will put all this from my mind, as you must from yours. To think too much about a problem is often far worse than not to think about it at all. The first brings no more than going over and over the same ground. The second may allow your mind to cleanse itself and see all difficulties afresh.'

Chapter Nineteen

A Phantom in the City

WHEN FOXE WAS IN NEED OF DISTRACTION, as he was the following morning, his thoughts turned at once to the Catt sisters. Whose turn was it for a visit? He decided it was Kitty's. After his normal breakfast, visit to the coffee house and walk around the Market Place, he therefore strode towards the theatre and Kitty's house nearby. The day matched his mood. There was a thin, cold rain and the muddy streets smelled of urine and horse dung.

Why did it matter that Bonneviot had been murdered? No one missed him. Others had dealt with the threat to the city's trade. Hinman's plan had failed. Why not leave all there?

Foxe found Kitty was risen and about, but she told him she had no time to spend with him that day. There was a evening's performance, in which she was playing the female lead. That required an afternoon of rehearsal, then a swift dinner, before returning to the theatre to dress and prepare.

Seeing his disappointment, Kitty took pity on him to the limited extent of exchanging several warm kisses. Then she told him to go to find if Gracie would see him, though she reminded him as he left that she kept most careful score of his visits to each of them.

'Come to me tomorrow, Ash,' she said. 'I will be free a good part of the day and you can make all up to me. I also have news of young George Bonneviot, which I think will interest you. Now, away to Gracie. If you do not make haste, she may already be planning to spend time leaving her card at various houses. Not all the fine ladies of this city are too blind to my sister's many virtues to see only the way she makes her living. Besides, more than a few learned the tricks that won them a wealthy husband from our Aunt Constance, when she was running the same establishment. They owe a debt that they are happy to repay.'

Gracie was not thus employed, but was to take tea later that afternoon with Mrs. Kendrew, a lady of great beauty and equal wealth. Lizzy Kendrew had once been amongst Gracie's girls. Then a rich and elderly customer had become besotted with her and whisked her off to a life of luxury. Being the most perfect gentleman, Mr. Kendrew had died within the year – from exhaustion, some said. Now his widow was rich and free to indulge a discreet taste for handsome young men whenever she wished.

Poor Foxe. His spirits sank very low, so that Gracie too took pity on him. She said she could allow him one hour, no more, and he was not to render her clothing as disordered, or absent, as he usually did. Being miserable, Foxe did not find this requirement too hard to accept. What he most wanted was comfort and Gracie, expert in the needs of men of all kinds, proved quick to give it.

Thus they cuddled together like an old married couple. Foxe rested his cheek on Gracie's soft bosom while she stroked his neck and crooned to him as a mother to her child. Foxe meanwhile, feeling most wonderfully soothed, poured out his tale of the Bonneviot affair.

'I am lost, Gracie. This whole affair has me completely befuddled. Now, I fear, we will never take Hinman. Even the faint hope that he might confess and explain everything is gone. All we know for certain is that Bonneviot is dead as a result of some conspiracy involving a man – Hinman – who is neither who nor what he said he was. It is most vexing. I begin to believe I should confess my failure and give up.'

'But the murderer should surely be brought to justice.'

'Perhaps. Yet all I have learned of Bonneviot tells me the world is well rid of the man.'

'It is not like you, Ash, to be so down-hearted. I am sure you will find out all in time.'

'At present, I cannot even find that wretch, Hinman.'

'I declare that man is like a phantom, Ash. It is almost as if he had never existed.'

The effect this innocent remark had on Foxe caused Gracie both surprise and alarm. He lay quite still against her for a moment. Then his entire body stiffened and he jumped and cried out. It was much as she had seen a man react when a severe electrical current was passed through his body in the course of a scientific demonstration.

'Gracie! Gracie! What a marvellous woman you are! That's the answer, but I was too dull to grasp it until you laid it out for me. I must go and think it all through. But first, I must thank you.'

Then, despite her calls for restraint and reminders of what she had told him but a few minutes ago, Foxe grasped her in his arms and kissed her many times. Only his recollection that she had less time free for him than he deemed necessary prevented him from going further.

As it was, he left her breathless, even if her clothing was still more or less in order.

Afterwards, Foxe could recall nothing of his walk back home. Nor his entry into the house. Nor Alfred's response to finding his master beaming like an idiot and demanding chocolate on the instant. Foxe's mind was so occupied by new thoughts and possibilities that nothing else could find a place.

What if Hinman never existed, he asked himself? What if he was indeed a phantom: a projection of an idea, conjured up to confuse those who looked on? He was most definitely not who he claimed to be – a man come from Halifax. Nor a wealthy entrepreneur engaged in worsted trading at home and overseas. Yet such a character was essential to the plot to gain entry to the offices of the leading master weavers of Norwich. Could he have been no more than an invention? A kind of puppet to conceal the man who had been manipulating this creation?

To what purpose? To conceal the true identity of the mastermind behind this whole affair. That went without saying. But was there no more to it than that? Why did this 'Hinman' spend so much time in the coffee houses and eating places of the city establishing the façade he had chosen? It must have possessed a greater importance in the business than just a means of concealment.

Thus Foxe reasoned with himself, going around and around the same ideas until his head ached and his shoulders were knotted and sore. He was on the cusp of discovering the whole nature of the affair, yet he could not make the final breakthrough. Certain essential pieces of information were still missing.

In the end, he stood up, stretched and called for Alfred to find young Charlie and send him with a message to Brock. Brock should wait on him the next morning upon his return from taking coffee. In the meantime, Foxe determined to enjoy his dinner and spend the evening at his club, indulging in a few games of cards and talking amiably to whoever he found there. Maybe, as before, turning his mind away from the problem would allow him the breakthrough he needed.

Mr. Foxe's evening at his club had proved pleasant, but failed to produce any fresh ideas in his mind. That was often how it went in matters of importance. For some time, nothing was clear and he made no progress. Then revelations came in torrents, leaving him scrambling to keep up. Yesterday, he believed that moment of the breaking open of this box of secrets had arrived. Today, he saw it had not.

Still, it was a fine morning and the air smelled fresher than it had been. Norwich was famous for the number and splendour of gardens within the city walls – a legacy of the Huguenot Strangers of a century back. Those poor refugees had also brought with them their other passion: the keeping of caged birds for their song. The Huguenot blood was now so intermingled with native ancestry that only certain family names, like Bonneviot, revealed its presence. Yet these other gifts had proved more permanent. On a morning such as this, you could imagine you caught the scent of flowers over the ranker smells of the street. And many a window contained a cage and fine canary-bird or two, filling the air with sweet singing.

Foxe sat at his normal table in The Swan and leaned back with a copy of one of the newspapers provided there. The news, alas, proved somewhat dull. Today it was little more that a bland recitation of political speeches and reports of the prospects for the year's harvest. Bored, Foxe turned to his other favourite pastime in that place, listening in to others' conversations.

To his left, three men were discussing the price of yarn in Ireland. Then they moved on to whether it might be possible to have more brought by sea directly to Yarmouth. To do so would avoid the costly process of landing the hanks at Bristol or Liverpool, then bringing them by road across the whole width of the realm. Foxe turned his attention elsewhere. That matter seemed of little interest to any but the many weavers about the place.

The two to his right were also talking business, but the nature of their topic proved both more interesting and more fruitful.

'I cannot understand him,' said the one. 'Does he need some new amount of capital? Does he need expertise lacking through any other means? I thought his brewery was prospering.'

'He told me he was finding the business too much of a burden to carry on alone,' the other replied. 'He has no son to succeed him. He may well hope by taking a partner to provide the means of realising the whole value of the business in time. He fears he may soon be no longer able to take an active part.'

'That I can well understand,' the first said. 'He must be not far short of his sixtieth year and has not been in good health of late. But could not he not find one in this city to join with him and perhaps take his place in a few years?'

'That I cannot say.'

'But this fellow he has now taken as a partner is a stranger to these parts. What does he know of him? You cannot ever have as secure a knowledge of someone from another place as you can of a local person. The wrong partner can break a business as easily as the right one can make it. I would have thought he should be more careful …'

Foxe stopped listening altogether at that point. His mind was, yet again, a maelstrom of thoughts and suppositions. He was amazed at his own credulity. Surely any sensible man would have been suspicious from the start of the idea that Bonneviot would take Hinman into business with him. Hinman was an unknown from another town, even if you believed his story of himself to be true. Bonneviot was quarrelsome and difficult, but no one had ever rated him a fool. Yet here he was, seemingly in a most difficult position following his falling-out with the Londoners, yet ready to engage with a person only lately arrived in Norwich. It made no sense! Any such deal would prove either the salvation or the undoing of Bonneviot's business. He may have been desperate, but even that could not account for such a piece of blatant stupidity. Who trusts all to an unknown?

There was another matter too. Bonneviot's executors, it seemed, had no firm knowledge of the nature or extent of the deal between Bonneviot and the supposed Mr. Hinman. No one did. The deal, all believed, had existed. What it was in detail, beyond having to do with selling the unsold stocks in Bonneviot's warehouse, remained shrouded in mystery. Was there no paperwork in Bonneviot's possession? Had he consulted no lawyer? Drawn up no contract between them? If such had existed, would not Hinman have produced it in support of his forged bill of sale?

Another thing. Bonneviot had arranged with Master Burford to sell his cloth on his behalf. Then they had all assumed that meant he planned to back out of his deal with Hinman. Yet the loan he had negotiated in London suggested otherwise. Wasn't it to finance him until the cloth could be sold, without any need for involvement with Hinman at all?

How on earth could all of this make sense? Surely Bonneviot must have believed Hinman had the funds needed to meet his share of the costs of the new operation? They knew now that was untrue, but Hinman would not have told Bonneviot that. If there was to be a deal, why back out while all still appeared well? Had he and the alderman been wrong in jumping to the conclusion that Bonneviot had somehow discovered Hinman planned to cheat him. But how? From whom? Before Bonneviot's murder, who would have doubted Hinman's claim to be able to sell cloth in large amounts? Would Bonneviot have reached a different conclusion?

No, the only way these matters could be turned into logic was to assume that Hinman and Bonneviot had probably not even met and that there had never been a deal planned between them. Bonneviot had always planned to ask Mr. Burford, and Mr. Burford alone, to help him out of his difficulty. This whole story of Hinman approaching Bonneviot and negotiating the supposed partnership was an invention – an elaborate smokescreen. It had been most cleverly built out of thin air, rumour and supposition. Once launched, the story was then spread about the coffee houses by a man who dressed, spoke and behaved in the best way to give credence to the invention.

Hinman had cozened them all, Foxe as much as the rest. Almost nothing of what they thought they knew was truth. They must sweep it aside and begin again.

Foxe put down his newspaper and was about to rise to leave his table, when another thought struck him.

Hold! Hold, he told himself. You are being led astray again. McSwiggan has confessed that it was Hinman who paid him to kill Bonneviot. But why? If there never was any deal between them, what reason could there be for Hinman wishing Bonneviot dead? The plan to use a forgery was, Foxe still believed, invented in haste to deal with the aftermath of Bonneviot's death. How would that square with Hinman being the man who arranged the murder? Would McSwiggan have killed Bonneviot on his own account? Would he then try to pass the blame to Hinman, when he realised he was the focus of an investigation? Surely that was to credit McSwiggan with more wit than he possessed. He had no reason to kill Bonneviot. It was through their need to secure the conviction of Hinman that they offered him inducement to turn King's Evidence. All MacSwiggan had to do to escape the gallows was to deny any involvement. Without his confession, vague stories of his drunken boasts were the best they could have produced as evidence. That would never have secured a conviction.

It was no use, Foxe could make no sense of it. The past two days had brought him a good many revelations and fresh ideas. Now all these had produced was still more confusion. He was beginning to doubt he knew anything for certain.

Thus returned to a state of gloom, Foxe left the coffee house and went home to talk with Brock. It took him a while to convince Brock too that they must doubt all the supposed facts that they had been relying upon. Now, when it was done, they stared at one another in dejection.

'I've no word of Hinman,' Brock said. 'Disappeared. Yet I know he was no ghost or spirit sent to torment us. No, he was flesh and blood, just as we are. I don't believe Beeston's men have found him either. They are still about the city, peering into corners and dragging folk out of their beds to see if he is hiding beneath.'

'He alone knows what this business has been about, Brock. What's worse, I believe he has been too clever for me.'

'There's still a chance …'

'Maybe, Brock, but it shrinks by the hour. And speaking of hours, I must keep my appointment with Kitty, though I fear she will find me a poor companion today. She has news of George Bonneviot, it seems. Now I must sound agog with interest and praise her for her efforts. Yet I believe he has either no part in this mystery or but a minor one.'

'Perhaps her news will surprise you. Perhaps she will tell you he is in league with Hinman and has spirited him away to London, or Paris, or Barbados.'

'Mocking me does not make me feel better, Brock, though I dare say I deserve it. When I asked her to discover what she could of George Bonneviot, I suspected he had some involvement in his father's death. Even then, all I thought I knew of the young man argued that he would never have the courage to undertake such a deed. At that time too, I knew little or nothing of the tangled matters of Bonneviot, the loan, the unsold cloth, Hinman, forgeries and Beeston. Poor George Bonneviot is now but a bystander, I fear. Still, Kitty may be able to clear up the small matter of where he is. I suppose I should be grateful for that.'

Chapter Twenty

Theatrical Parts

'DEAR ASH,' KITTY SAID. 'HOW PROMPT YOU ARE! All eager to hear my news, I expect. Sit down, then. Now, before I begin, I must alas dash any other hopes you might have for coming to see me today. I am engaged to take tea with Lady Rootham and her friends at four and have yet to dress for the occasion. Lady Rootham's party came to the theatre last evening and were much affected by my performance. They came to my dressing-room afterwards to offer their congratulations. Then they invited me to take tea with them today.'

'Is that THE Lady Rootham?' Foxe said. 'I ask merely to know who it is who has taken my place.'

'Jealousy does not become you, my dear. Yes, so far as I know, there is only one person of that name in this county.'

'Thus jealousy seems quite appropriate.'

'I am well aware that the lady in question has in the past shown herself partial to beautiful young ladies, Ash. I am intrigued by her. She might also be a useful patroness of my career. But do you not think me able to defend my honour, should that become necessary?'

'Most able, Kitty, if not always most willing.'

Kitty treated him to one of her tinkling, trademark giggles. 'I assure you, she may be of a certain persuasion, but I believe I have often given you enough proof that I have little inclination to take that path. No, I am flattered and curious, nothing more.'

'The more you play the part of the artless ingenue, the more I suspect I am being taken in. But I am not jealous, save only that she has taken you from me today.'

'That, I assure you, I will put right soon, even if you did spend your time with my sister so chastely yesterday.'

Foxe wondered whether the two ever had any other topic of conversation than comparing his actions towards the other, but let it pass. Kitty was in a playful mood and would enjoy tormenting him She might even forget what he had come to hear.

'George Bonneviot,' he said. 'You said you had word of him.'

'George Bonneviot. Yes, you asked me to find out what I could. I flatter myself that I have done well enough. I believe I told you before that I thought he had approached all the Norwich acting companies and the managers had turned him away.'

'Yes, that is what I recall.'

'It seems the principal reason was the same in each case. They knew of his father's disapproval of the son's wish to become an actor. They also knew the family's wealth and George's position as the only son and heir. Managers soon become sick of rich young men who are stage-struck and wish to act. Few have any talent. Even fewer possess the willingness to undertake all the hard work required. Most assume within a week or so their name will be at the head of the bill. All these want to do is brag to their friends and fumble the actresses. If they are taken on, it is not long before they tire of the business and return to their homes and the family fortune.'

'And young George was of this kind?'

'So they assumed, for none gave him any chance to show otherwise. They turned him away, with vague suggestions of perhaps seeking out one of the London companies.'

'So what did he do?' Foxe asked.

'What they told him to do. He went to London. Since none knew him there, he found one or two willing to let him at least take part in a rehearsal.' Kitty smiled. 'The London managers are notorious for their practical jokes on aspiring artists. I am sure they thought to have a rare time watching a raw amateur make a fool of himself.'

'Did he?'

'By no means. As I was told, he acquitted himself bravely. Of course, he had little of the craft needed, but enough talent showing to make them change their tune and begin to take him seriously. Yet still none would take him on.'

'Why was that?'

'London audiences are the most unforgiving in the world. Oh, if you are a young and pretty actress, as I was then …'

'And still are,' Foxe said at once, so that Kitty rewarded him with a dazzling smile and a blown kiss.

'… they will tolerate you, just so long as you show them enough of your charms and remain a novelty. But when they have seen all they can, they tire of the game. Then they are quick enough to hiss and drive you from the stage – throwing things, if need be.'

'It is no place to learn your craft, then.'

'The worst. A young man seeking to do more than bear a spear or speak a single line would have a hard time of it. Nor would the company manager escape unscathed. If the common populace did not wreck his performances, his rivals would send their hired bands to hiss and shout and cause a riot. To be a successful theatre manager in London is to be the object of ferocious jealousy from all the others.'

'They told him this?'

'Not perhaps as I have told you, but yes. They gave him encouraging words and advised him to seek out some provincial company. There he might learn his stage-craft and in time gain the presence to stand before a London audience. Small provincial theatres are the best training grounds, Ash. Most change their repertoire often, putting on different programmes each night of their stay in a town. You might be playing a tyrant on a Tuesday, a melting lover on Wednesday and a noble prince on Thursday. As well, of course, as all manner of other parts in the farces and recitations that fill up the evening.'

'I can see that you must gain experience quickly by such means.'

'Not just experience, confidence too. Most actors feel great apprehension before taking the stage. Will you forget your lines or miss a cue? Will you stumble? Move to stage right when you should go stage left? To stand before hundreds of people while they laugh at you – unless that is the object of your part – is the most mortifying of events. And if you are playing a comic role, yet none laugh, you wish the stage to open and drag you out of sight.'

'Is it so bad? Even for you?'

'Especially for someone like me, Ash. I am well known and have a reputation, yet every time I stand before an audience I am risking all again. Have you never remarked to a friend that Mrs. So-and-so is not perhaps what she once was? Or that some famous comedian's timing seems to have deserted him more often than it did? Such remarks, should the person mentioned overhear them, are as sharp as the slash of a sword.'

'My poor darling!'

'What gets you through all is confidence: the ability to take the blows and cat-calls, yet still carry on. Once lose that and your career is over.'

'I can see well that I have underestimated you, Kitty. I never doubted your ability and talent, nor your beauty. But I have been woefully ignorant of the determination you must show to survive, let alone shine as you do. I doubt our George would have been up to it.'

'Then you would be wrong. It seems he lost little of his enthusiasm when they told him to look elsewhere. Indeed, he accepted the advice and left London at once to seek out a company willing to allow him to learn with them. It seems we have all underestimated that young man.'

'I must own myself the most guilty of all. From what little I learned of him, I had built a picture of a feeble, languid young dandy. I believed him ever ready to blame his lack of achievement on the faults of others. But do you know where he went?'

'All I could learn was that he went to the north. Some said Richmond, some Harrogate and one York. It may have been any of those.'

'And he is still there?'

'So far as any knows. Not even the most talented of learners could aspire to join a company in London without five years or more experience in good provincial work. You might need three years' proper training even to gain a place in an acting company in a great city such as Norwich.'

'I wonder if he met Hinman in those parts?' Foxe mused to himself. 'He claimed to come from Halifax, which is not, I believe, so far away. That could explain how he had heard of Bonneviot senior. It may even have been before he arrived here.'

'What are you mumbling about, Ash? Have I not done well enough for you? Do I not deserve my round of applause?'

'Most assuredly, Kitty! My humblest apologies. I was merely pondering a possible link. No, you have been as brilliant as I could have hoped, and you deserve full tribute for it.'

Foxe stood up at once and clapped his hands, calling out 'Bravo!' several times for good measure. Then he darted forward and kissed Kitty half a dozen times with increasing warmth and ardour.

'No! No, sir! However much you make trial of my resolution, I must stand firm. Nor would I submit to your embraces without the time to enjoy them to the full. Let me go, I say! Enough! It will never do to arrive at Lady Rootham's home late or in less than my full finery. Please, Ash! You know I do not send you away willingly, especially when you kiss me thus … nor when you do that with your hand. Have pity!'

Foxe stood back a little and dropped his hands to his side. 'See, I am all goodness,' he said, laughing all the while. 'Go to your Sapphic lover.'

'Do not say so! Not even in jest. I will not have you putting it about that I might submit to any such relationship. Think of my reputation.'

'As the most shameless little minx and hussy in Norwich … and the prettiest? Very well. You must soon prove the truth of your claims most fully to make me hold my tongue.'

'As you know I will, Ash … and perhaps more fully than you can imagine, for you make me wish to drive you to eat your teasing words. I will speak with my sister, I think, and ask her to help me devise a suitable punishment …'

'Mercy! Mercy!,' Foxe cried at once. 'If the two of you plot against me, I will have no chance. You know I am but tweaking your tail a little.'

'Ah, but you are the one with the tail that might best be tweaked, though it hang in front rather than behind.'

'Kitty!'

'Ah, now the teasing is directed at you, it is another matter. Off you go, Ash, before I decide to make good my threats at once. Be sure the punishment is but postponed. I will not forget what I owe you. Nor the proofs you have so ungallantly demanded of me. You will pay in full, I promise. In full!'

As Foxe made his escape, he reflected happily on his skill as an actor in convincing Kitty that he valued what she had discovered for him. The worth of the discoveries themselves he doubted. He had indeed been wrong about George Bonneviot. Yet it could matter little. If he was somewhere amongst Yorkshire theatrical folk and ever on the road, it was quite likely he had not yet heard of his father's death. It would not count for much when he did. He had not long past been sent packing from his home, with but a few pounds in his hand. He also had the sure knowledge that there would be no inheritance for him to look forward to.

Foxe spent the rest of the day dealing with domestic and business matters. He had to make up his accounts and render payments to various traders and those who supplied his home with food and coals. There were small items of correspondence to be dealt with as well. He generally found such matters soothing to his mind, but today it seemed nothing could bring him the rest he craved.

Even late into the evening, he felt restless and disordered. It was as if something was scratching at his consciousness, yet always just out of his mind's reach. He tried to read, but found himself looking over the same page a dozen times before he could recall any of its content. When he attempted to compose a letter, the words danced upon the page and became entangled in such labyrinthine complexity none could have followed his meaning. At length, he gave up all occupation. He sat in his chair, staring into some distant place, while his brain filled with fog and his feet and legs grew colder by the minute.

At ten, he went to his bed, though he was sure he would not be able to sleep. In fact, he fell into a heavy slumber within but a few minutes. Yet even then, his mind could not be stilled completely. He experienced a tumbling mass of incoherent dreams that rendered him tense and afraid. Finally, he awoke with a great start. Some old woman was prowling at the foot of the bed and running her clammy hands around his feet and ankles. But that too was a dream. He had proved so restless that the covers had slid to one side, leaving his feet sticking out into the cold of the bedroom.

At this point, he grew disgusted with himself and determined to abandon any idea of further sleep. Instead, he would make a thorough revision of all he knew about the death of Bonneviot. He still felt he was on the edge of discovering those key facts that would make sense of the matter.

Hinman did not exist. That was clear. That character was a mere phantom, conjured up to conceal the identity of the one he must assume was behind the whole business. But why? Who could that genuine person be? Such an elaborate deception must have had some important purpose.

Round and round his mind went. He heard the church clocks chime three or four times. He heard the watchman's clapper. He even heard – or thought he did – the first birdsong.

Then he had it! Nothing else could explain the extent and depth of the charade that produced Mr. Hinman. It could only be necessary for one reason. The man behind it must be well-known in the city! A genuine stranger would have little need to conceal his identity. He might assume a false name. He might even try to appear richer, or more honest, or even more experienced in matters of the cloth trade than he was. But there would have been no call for him to spend so many hours and days convincing all he met that he was Mr. Hinman of Halifax. Hinman must be someone who would otherwise have been easily known. He had to stay incognito. His whole plan must have turned on that. But why?

The deal with Bonneviot to sell his stocks of cloth overseas had also never existed. It too was an illusion, most cunningly produced from hints, assumptions and rumour. Why was that necessary? Until that night he realised he had never even asked himself that question. He had begun by believing in the supposed deal, like everyone else. Yet even when he suspected it was a falsehood, he had failed to ask why.

He laid it all out for himself again. The character of Hinman had been invented to conceal the identity of one who must otherwise be know to all. The matter of the deal with Bonneviot had also been made up, this time to hide the true purpose of the conspiracy. But if that plot had not been to persuade Bonneviot to enter a binding arrangement with Hinman, what was it for?

Oh, Good Lord! What if it had only ever been about seizing ownership of those specific bales of cloth? The ones that were already known to be stored, unsold, in Bonneviot's warehouse?

Why had Hinman, whoever he was, been so insistent that the fake bill of sale be dated exactly three weeks before it was forged? It must, of course, have born a date before Bonneviot's death. Yet why that precise date? Had the mastermind known about the real arrangement with Master Burford? Had he wished his counterfeit contract to appear to have been made before the genuine deal had taken place? Yet how had he known, when no one else save Bonneviot and Burford were aware of it? And why did he allow that arrangement to proceed, since it had already resulted in the sale of some of the cloth he was trying to steal?

Foxe could not believe that Hinman had known of Burford. If he had, he could have brought about Bonneviot's death earlier, thus removing any complications to his claim to be the prior owner of the cloth. Bonneviot had to die to stop him from denying the authenticity of the bill of sale. That was clear. They had all assumed that his death had been arranged only after Hinman had arrived in the city and somehow learned of the unsold stocks of cloth. But if Hinman was, in reality, a local man, he could have been present the whole time. The delay between learning of Bonneviot's problems and arranging the conspiracy would be accounted for by the time it must have taken to set all in motion.

He had to find a forger, an assassin and establish the credibility of Hinman's identity. Only then could he move forward. He had also needed to get money from Beeston. Don't forget that, Foxe told himself. His need for cash to support his deception proved that, whoever he was, he was not a wealthy man. Perhaps he was a weaver whom Bonneviot cheated out of his wages and planned this elaborate revenge? It was difficult to believe that an artisan could have been able to bring off such a deception. Especially since it demanded he should pass himself off as a person of some means. Could a mere weaver have convinced the entire city that he was either the younger son of a gentleman, or at least one of the middling sort? Could he have paid someone else to do it for him?

Foxe decided that the only way to resolve such matters would be to speak with the alderman as soon as possible. He might at least be able to suggest persons capable of passing themselves off as Hinman. It seemed they had little enough chance of laying hands on the man himself. If Beeston reached him first, he might not even survive to tell his tale. If not, he would probably get clean away. They must rely on their own resources to solve the mystery, even if that meant their answer could never be more than the product of careful reasoning and educated guesswork.

Rising from his bed, Foxe lit a candle, wrapped himself in a warm dressing-gown, found his slippers and made his way downstairs. No sense in waking the rest of the house. When he reached his study, he found paper and pen to write two notes that Alfred should deliver that morning. Then he returned to his room, got back into bed and slept most peacefully, untroubled by worries or dreams.

Chapter Twenty-One

Death and Illumination

FOXE AWOKE WITH THE UNEASY SENSE that someone was standing by his bed. He opened one eye, then two. The presence by the bed was Alfred, who appeared uncertain whether he should shake his master awake or make a noise to attract his attention.

'Alfred?' Foxe mumbled. 'What time is it?'

'A little after seven, Master. Mr. Brock is downstairs and was most insistent that I come to wake you.'

'Brock? At this hour? Whatever for?'

'That I do not know. He came to the back door about five minutes ago. Fortunately, Mrs. Dobbins and the maid were already about and had lit the kitchen fire. I believe they have made him coffee, Master. Would you like me to bring you some?'

By this time, Foxe was – at last – awake. He rarely rose so early and was quite unused to the pale light in his room and the pervading sense of chill. His small fire had gone out hours ago. The maid would usually make it up and light it again in good time to warm the room before he ventured from his bed.

'No, Alfred. I will take it in the dining room. If Brock is here so early, he must be the bearer of bad news. Tell him that I will be down shortly. Then find me the warmest dressing gown you can – and my slippers. Confound it all! I should have another hour or more of sleep before me, at least. Oh … another matter, Alfred. You will find two notes on the desk in my study. Please have them delivered as soon as possible.'

'Yes, Master.'

'Just one more thing, Alfred. Is the fire in the dining room lit?'

'I will attend to that myself, as soon as I have informed Mr. Brock of your wishes. The heavy curtains there seem to hold in the warmth. It is not so cold as it is here. Do you wish to wash and shave before coming down, Master?'

'No. Brock will have to take me as I am. Now, away to light that fire!'

True to his word, Foxe came into the dining room in scarcely more than the five minutes he had promised. There he found Brock seated at the table, staring into a half-empty dish of coffee and looking even more miserable than usual.

Foxe held up a hand to prevent Brock from coming out with his news at once, whatever it was. He needed first to sit down and drink some coffee. Such an early start was a severe shock to his system. Since Brock's face seemed to presage yet more upsets, he needed to prepare himself.

At length, after he had drunk a whole dish of Mrs. Dobbins' excellent coffee, he signed to Brock that he might begin.

'Beeston got to 'im first, Foxe, as I feared 'e would. The constables found 'im about first light, face down on a dung-heap at the end of some filthy alley near the river.'

'Dead?'

'As a brass doornail. One of the constables is an acquaintance of mine. He knew I was seeking the man, so 'e sent word as soon as 'e could.'

'We are talking of Hinman?'

'We are. I've seen the body. It's 'im, right enough. By the look of 'im, Beeston had 'is men encourage 'im to explain himself first. Then, probably because the explanation was not to Beeston's liking, they were let loose to exact punishment. Hinman wasn't a heavily-built man, Foxe, nor one used to rough treatment, I'd say. Whether their actions were meant to kill 'im, I couldn't tell you. That they did is plain enough on his body.'

'So. That is an end of it.'

'Is that all you have to say? I still clung to the hope that we might somehow find him first. That's why I've been scouring this city night and day. This wretched business 'as caused me more loss of sleep than enough. Now I'm never to know what it was all about.'

'Be of good cheer, Brock. Hinman may be dead, but I still hope to find the answer. Now, sit quiet and drink some more coffee. I have a letter to write. Alfred!'

Foxe suspected his man would not be far away. He was proved correct, for Alfred came in almost on the instant.

'Your papers are on their way, master.'

'Excellent. Now bring me paper, pen and ink. Then, when I have written this further letter, be ready to take it yourself to the address I will give you. It must reach the person to whom it is addressed as quickly as possible.'

Brock stared, unable to reason why Foxe was so calm in the face of what seemed to him to be the wreck of all their plans. Now, while he waited for the letter to be finished and Alfred sent on his way with it, Foxe asked him another question he could not have expected.

'Do you know where the constables have taken Hinman's body, Brock?'

'Um … think so. Yes … that's right. One of 'em said they'd take it to the undercroft of The Guildhall. It's cool there all year. I don't imagine the coroner will hasten from his bed to see the corpse of someone who's a stranger to the city.'

'No, I don't imagine he will. Nor would he have done for a local man. Unless the dead man had been the mayor himself. Maybe not even then. Once you are dead, you stay dead, so haste is not necessary. Good, good. That works to our favour …' Foxe bent his head and returned to writing his letter. A few moments later, he looked up and beckoned Alfred over.

'Right, Alfred. Please bear this with all speed to the coroner's house. Tell whichever servant takes it in that I am awaiting his or her master's reply with great eagerness. He is like to take all day about the matter otherwise. If whoever takes in the letter still seems reluctant to make haste, you may add that the mayor is being informed of its contents. He will be angry should the matters within not be set in motion as quickly as may be.'

None of this made any sense to poor Brock, but it seemed his friend was not in a mood to explain himself.

'Now, Brock,' Foxe said. 'I am in need of breakfast, early though it is. I am sure that Mrs. Dobbins has already anticipated my wishes in the matter, so be so good as to pull the bell for the maid. We will eat together.'

Before Brock could even rise from his chair, they heard a knocking on the front door of the house and the maid hastening to see who else could be calling at such an hour. There was a sound of low voices, then the girl herself came into the room with a letter on a small tray.

'Beg pardon, Master. But seein' Mr. Alfred is absent and the alderman's man said this 'ere note was most urgent, I thought as 'ow I should bring it right away.'

'You thought rightly, Molly. Thank you. When you return to the kitchen, please ask Mrs. Dobbins to send breakfast for myself and Mr. Brock as soon as she may.'

'She 'ad it almost ready when I left 'er, Master, so I'll be bringin' it soon enough, I dare say.'

Foxe looked at the letter before him and gave a great sigh. 'It seems to be a day for surprises, Brock. Let us hope this one at least does not involve death. I doubt the alderman will even have heard of Hinman's murder, so it cannot be about that.'

Quickly he opened the letter and scanned the contents. Then, to Brock's total amazement, he let out what sounded like a cry of triumph.

'I was right, Brock. This proves it. See! The alderman writes that he has spoken himself with a good many of the master weavers of the city and sent messages to the rest. The final reply came late last evening, so he must have written this before he retired to bed and told a servant to deliver it first thing. I cannot see our worthy alderman being about at ... what is it?' Foxe peered at the clock on the shelf above the grate. ' ... a quarter to eight in the morning.'

'You're the most irritating of men sometimes, Foxe,' Brock growled. 'I rush 'ere bearing what seems to me the worst news possible in this affair and you seem barely interested. Then you sit and write a letter, saying nothing to me of the contents, and calmly call for your breakfast. Now you yell like an excited child and still tell me nothing of what's in your mind. It's enough to make a man run mad.'

'Ah, my humblest apologies, good Brock. I am too wont to assume that what I see must be plain to all, though there is no way that you could work out why I am not cast down by your news. Nor see what the alderman has written as proof that I am right in my reasoning.'

'For Heaven's sake, man, stop talking in riddles and tell me plainly what is going on.'

Foxe smiled at his friend and waved the letter towards him. 'First, Alderman Halloran writes that Hinman approached no one amongst the master weavers save Bonneviot. None had even heard of him. He has no idea what to make of this.'

'But you have, it seems.'

'Indeed I have, Brock. I had guessed as much last night, after a long time of going over and over the matter in my head. Now I am certain that this whole affair has been aimed solely at Bonneviot from the start. All the rest was a smoke-screen to hide this fact. Someone wanted to seize as much of Bonneviot's wealth as he could. He also needed to do so before the falling-out with the Londoners could see it much diminished, or even lost.'

At that moment, Foxe fell silent. He stared at Brock without seeing him. He clapped his hand to his head and let out another yell that made poor Brock start from his chair. Even Mrs. Dobbins came from the kitchen to see what might be amiss.

'What a devilish cunning plan, Brock! What daring and determination! It all makes perfect sense. Oh, it would be beautiful, if it were not aimed at murder. There is just one piece missing, which I must deal with at once. Mrs. Dobbins! I am glad you are here. Has Alfred returned?'

'Not yet, Master. But are you well? I thought I heard you cry out.'

'Never better! Now, you will have to take Alfred's place. Find young Charlie Dillon. He may be hanging around outside already, for he has the best nose for business I ever encountered. Have him ready to take a note to Miss Kitty with all the speed he can muster. She will not be awake at this hour, but he is to insist that her maid give her the note at once. Then he is to wait for her reply and bear it back to me as fast as his young legs will carry him. Tell him it is worth a whole shilling, if he be but quick. Now where is that pen ...?'

Mrs. Dobbins and Brock exchanged looks that said clearly they might both esteem Mr. Foxe greatly, but neither would ever fathom the full extent of his oddities. Then, as Mrs. Dobbins hurried away, her master called her back.

'One more thing, Mrs. Dobbins. Send Charlie first to take my letter to Miss Kitty and bring back her reply. Then tell him he is to go to the alderman's house and ask if I might might call there tomorrow morning at eleven o'clock. Let him add that the mystery is solved and I will explain all when I come.'

Brock was struck dumb at that last part. He sat with his mouth hanging open and his eyes wide with wonder.

'Cheer up, Brock! All we have to do now is wait. Ah, Molly. What a brace of treasures you and Mrs. Dobbins are. Breakfast! I have not been so hungry in many a long year. Now, set all on the table and I will try to persuade my friend here to use his open mouth for its proper use by filling it with food. Fresh coffee too, girl! Quick as you can.' Then, with a broad wink at Brock, he set to and began to eat.

The alderman replied swiftly to Foxe's message. Indeed, Foxe and Brock had barely finished their breakfasts when the note arrived. They would be expected at eleven the next day. The mayor and the Master of the Weaver's Guild would also be present, for all were eager to learn what Foxe had discovered.

Charlie Dillon had also brought back a verbal message from Miss Kitty. 'She says to tell you two things,' he said, trying and failing to conceal a mighty grin as he did so. 'The answer to your question is about two years or more past. The other is that if you ever demand she be woken again for such a silly matter as this, she'll forbid you 'er 'ouse. I don't think as 'ow she meant it, Mr. Foxe. She were smiling too much.'

'Perhaps you are right, though I will not take the risk, save in a matter as important as this. I see that you are already learning the ways of women, Charlie. If you continue thus, in a few years you will become a terrible temptation to their whole sex, I fear. Now, here is your shilling, just as I promised. Alas, this affair is almost at an end, so you will have no need to be on call outside so much of the time.'

'Thass all right, Mr. Foxe. It were good while it lasted and I'm sure you'll 'ave some other caper goin' afore long.'

'That young man's too sharp,' Brock said, after Charlie had left. 'I wonder he ain't cut 'is own throat before now.'

'I only wish I could persuade him to get some schooling,' Foxe said. 'I would pay willingly, but there … he would wilt in such an environment. Now, Brock, you must come with me tomorrow to the alderman's house.'

'I was afraid you'd say that. Do I have too? You know these rich types make me uneasy.'

'They are no better than you, Brock. Maybe worse. They just have money, which usually says as much about their fathers as it does about them. You must be there. You have been an essential part of the unravelling of this mystery from the start. Just dress a little more tidily than usual and I am sure they will scarce notice you.'

'But they're rich merchants and the like, and I was only ever the man who sailed a wherry up and down to Yarmouth!'

'Without you, and those like you, Brock, their businesses would soon have fallen into ruin. Until you had that accident, you were the best captain on the river. Now you and I are owners of the most wherries. You have helped build a fine business, though others had to take your place on board. How many wherries do we own now?'

'Six … no, seven … eight.'

'There you are. You have been as successful as they. Now, no more complaints. Come here at a suitable time and we will walk to the alderman's house together.'

'Can't you tell me what you know now, Foxe? That message from Kitty made your face light up, but I couldn't make head nor tail of it.'

'Patience, my friend. I have yet to hear from the coroner to make my enquiries complete. Tomorrow you will know all, I promise. Now, off with you about your business. I have to get my thoughts into their proper order, if I am to convince the mayor and his colleagues.'

Around an hour later, Foxe had received replies to both of the notes he had asked Alfred to deliver that morning. As he read the final one, he smiled. Mrs. Bonneviot had provided the very last piece in the puzzle.

Chapter Twenty-Two

Foxe's Tale

FOXE, BROCK AND HIS OTHER GUESTS WERE GATHERED next morning in Alderman Halloran's fine new library. He was so proud of it. He was still more proud of some of the books collected there. Since many had passed through Foxe's hands before finding a resting-place on the shelves, Foxe was quite proud of it too. Brock had, as requested, come in his best clothes. They may have been sombre in comparison with what Foxe was wearing, but no one – least of all three leaders of the textile trade – could miss the quality of the cloth and the cut.

Mr. Foxe was resplendent. His dark maroon frock-coat was adorned with embroidered flowers and leaves, picked out with gold threads. The coat was then edged with an intricate pattern of acanthus and fastened with gilded and enamelled buttons. His breeches were in a matching cloth and were decorated in similar style. He wore a waist-coat of glistening white silk brocade, though it was hard to see the fabric for the dense embroideries in silver wire that covered the surface. Its buttons were also silver, though each had upon it a neat pattern of small diamonds and sapphires. His stockings were finest white silk and his shoes made of flowered brocade, with diamond and silver buckles. He was even wearing his newest and finest wig. These great men of the city – though each was sporting his own finery – were quite eclipsed by his magnificence.

The three worthies greeted this apparition solemnly, then Alderman Halloran turned to Brock and extended the welcome to him.

'Mr. Brock – nay, Captain Brock! I am delighted to see you in my house, sir. You must know the mayor and the Master here, for they know you, I am sure. Your wherries are amongst the best and most reliable on our river. We were all sad when you were forced to leave your post on the deck. Yet I know that your business has prospered since then, so perhaps Providence worked its mysterious ways to the good. Sit down, gentlemen! We are agog to hear your news, but you must, I beg you, take some coffee or chocolate first. Mr. Mayor? Master? Good. I will ring for the maid.'

As politeness demanded, all sipped their drinks and engaged in light conversation. Meanwhile, the air hummed with tense anticipation for what was to come. Eventually, the alderman put down his dish, glanced at his guests and turned to Foxe.

'We are all ready, Foxe. If it is agreeable to you, please begin.'

Foxe put down his empty coffee dish, took a deep breath and looked at his expectant audience. He was as sure as he might be that he had solved the mystery. Still, he could not help feeling some nervousness. To the world at large, there had never been anything to take note of beyond the sad murder of an eminent master weaver by some footpad. The people in this room alone would know the full extent of the conspiracy, and only he could tell them how it had unfolded and point to the events and characters who had brought it about.

'We must begin at the beginning,' Foxe said, 'and that was some years ago.' This was the first surprise. The mayor and the Master looked at one another in alarm. All these events had taken place within the last month. Why was Foxe delving so far into the past?

'The roots of this mystery reach back some thirteen years,' Foxe said. 'That was when Daniel Bonneviot decided that his only son, George, had received more than enough schooling. He should now be prepared to succeed his father as a master weaver. Bonneviot decided to send him to London, as his father had done with him. There he would serve his apprenticeship with a relative. Daniel had served under an uncle. George was to serve one of his father's cousins. George was twelve.'

'That's about the usual age to start an apprenticeship,' the Master commented. 'Nothing strange so far.'

'Late yesterday evening I received some information I had asked for from Mrs. Eliza Swan, Daniel Bonneviot's daughter and George's step-sister. It adds something essential to this tale.' Foxe refused to be put off his stride. 'George was adamant, even then, that he had no interest in the weaving trade or an apprenticeship. He wished to continue his schooling. It seems he was always quite a bookish lad. His father, being a perfect tyrant to all his family, would listen to no opposition. He decided everything. Others around him were expected to submit to his will on the instant.'

The other men looked at each other. This was, perhaps, a little extreme, but most fathers expected to be obeyed in major matters.

'George fell ill, perhaps as a result of his father's bullying. Ill enough for the move to London to be delayed by a full year. Still Daniel was adamant that he would be obeyed, so young George was despatched the next year to live with his new master. According to his step-sister, this man offered his new apprentice greater kindness and indulgence than he, George, had received at home. Perhaps that was why George stayed and duly completed his apprenticeship. I do not know. What I do know is that sometime during his stay in London, George discovered the theatre. Soon he became certain that his future lay in that direction.'

'The theatre!' The mayor had only contempt for such a futile business as the theatre.

'Indeed. Now a fully-fledged journeyman weaver, George returned home for the first time in seven years. What passed between him and his father I cannot say. Mrs. Swan was married by then and no longer privy to what went on in her father's household. I imagine George must, once again, have refused to take up the work his father expected of him. I do know that he went the rounds of the Norwich acting companies, trying to find a place with one of them. All turned him away. They had no room for a young man they saw as the dilettante son of a wealthy merchant. Perhaps they also feared reprisals from his father. Whatever the reason, they suggested Daniel try his luck in London. So that is what he did. This brief and unsatisfactory return home was about two years ago. As a result, George went back to London, determined to begin an acting career.'

'And his father allowed this?' Alderman Halloran asked.

'Again, I do not know. It may be that his father assumed the plan to be no more than youthful rebellion. Perhaps he was sure George would meet the same rebuff in London as he had in Norwich, and be forced back into obedience by that route. In once sense he was correct. No London manager would take the lad. This time, their reason was a good one: London audiences can be cruel and it is no place to learn your stagecraft. Yet they were prepared to allow George to take part in rehearsals and by this means confirmed his real talent. So they advised him to seek out some provincial company to train with. Once again, George left London. This time he went north, probably to Richmond or Harrogate in Yorkshire. There he found what he sought and began to act.'

'So he was in the north when his father was killed?' Brock said.

'That is what we all assumed. I must own to making too many mistakes in understanding this matter. First I accepted the tale, doubtless coming from Bonneviot senior, that George was a limp young man, unwilling to apply himself. Now I find he possessed all the determination and strength of purpose that both his father and grandfather had shown.'

'The old man, Jerome Bonneviot, was totally pig-headed,' the Master commented. 'You could no more move him from his purpose than shift our cathedral a mile up-river. I encountered him as a young man and he terrified me.'

'My second mistake was to assume that George's return to Norwich and attempt to find work in the theatre here was of recent date. If so, the time needed to return to London, be turned away again – kindly, this time – and go to the north must mean he was far, far away when his father died. I recall commenting to you, Brock, that he may not yet have heard of the death.'

'You did say that, as I recall. And I agreed with you.'

'Now I know two years or more had passed since he left Norwich. Was he still in the north?'

'Was he?' the mayor asked.

'No, sir. I must make some guesses here, but I am sure I will not be too far from the truth. I believe that recently – say four weeks ago – George returned home to see his father. I suspect he was doing well in his new career. Maybe he even had an opportunity to go to London and take a major part there. Whatever the occasion, he was proud of what he had achieved. Now he came to point out to his father that he had made good, though Daniel Bonneviot had always doubted him. It was what happened next that caused all the other elements in this mystery.'

Foxe's audience were silent now, completely caught up in the drama unfolding before them.

'Far from being pleased, we know that Daniel Bonneviot was enraged. He thrust a note for a hundred pounds into his son's hand, told him that was all the inheritance he would ever get and forbade him the house. George was to be cut-off totally. So much is certain. The next is conjecture, but I am sure again that it is not far from the truth. Someone told George about his father's quarrel with the London merchants. He also learned of the unsold cloth piling up in the warehouse. Maybe he guessed his father was existing only on the basis of loans. He would certainly hear that Bonneviot was laying off out-workers and delaying payments where ever he might. That was the common talk of the town. George knew his father only too well. He knew Daniel would never be willing to admit a mistake or back down. He must have realised that, without some change, the business and the family fortune was in gravest danger.'

'That must have been a shock indeed,' the alderman said.

'I am sure it was. Of course, we know now that Daniel Bonneviot had made a secret deal with Master Burford, but I am sure George could not have known that. Perhaps it had not even been completed at that time. All he would see was a business headed for bankruptcy, due to his father's stubbornness and temper.'

'But he had been disinherited!' The mayor seemed to be struggling to keep up with these revelations. 'It would no longer matter to him.'

'No, indeed. But it would plunge his mother into poverty and cause great hardship to many loyal workers. I know from my conversation with Mrs. Swan that she felt little love for her father. All her life, she had been forced to bow to his will and take on roles she did not want to follow. I also know from elsewhere …' Foxe carefully avoided mentioning that his source had been Mistress Gracie Catt. ' … that Bonneviot seemed to take pleasure in violence directed at women. It seems likely to me that both his wives, and his daughter too, had suffered many blows and indignities at his hands. Now George discovered, so he believed, that his father was prepared to ruin his whole family to pursue a foolish quarrel with London merchants. It was the last straw. He had to be stopped.'

While the rest sat silent, absorbing what Foxe had told them, the mayor was still some way behind.

'Stopped? How could George stop him? He was disinherited. He had no standing from which to launch a court action, nor any sway with his father that might let him try persuasion.'

'Bonneviot had to die. Then George had to find a way to claim the unsold cloth, since he could not inherit it. Once it was his, he would sell it and make money enough to support his mother and give him the inheritance so unjustly denied him. The plan was laid. All that was needed was a way to lure his father to a specific place at a specific time, where the hired assassin would be waiting.'

'No! No! I am lost, sir,' the mayor protested. 'George did not kill his father, Hinman did. George did not claim the cloth, that was Hinman too. George was disinherited. He could not claim anything.'

'George Bonneviot and Hinman were one and the same person,' Brock said. 'Am I not right, Foxe?'

'You are, Brock. In what transpired, we have the greatest possible proof of George Bonneviot's talents as an actor. Aye, and a playwright too, for he it was who wrote and staged the melodrama that was to unfold before us all.'

There was silence. The mayor appeared completely stunned, while the alderman and Guild Master frowned in violent concentration. Was there truly a wholly new explanation for what they thought they had once understood?

'Jerome Bonneviot had collected books,' Foxe continued at last. 'After his death, his son, Daniel, sold them. Not all at once. He sold them in small lots whenever he needed extra cash. By now, nearly all were gone, yet he still had a few worth selling. I asked Mrs. Bonneviot if she had known of her husband's gradual sale of his father's collection. She has written to tell me that she did. He made no secret of it.'

'What …? Books? How do books feature here?' It was the mayor again. His face was becoming red with the effort of keeping up.

'George must also have known what his father did when money was tight. Now, I believe, he sent word to Daniel Bonneviot – posing as Mr. James Hinman, I expect – expressing an interest in purchasing certain books he must have known for sure were in his grandfather's collection. I imagine he suggested a price large enough to cause Daniel to rush to sell them without further thought. The only stipulation was that the sale should be secret. Mr. Hinman specified the exact time and place. There he would receive the books and hand over the money.'

'Were these books so valuable …?', Alderman Halloran said. Then his face showed he had grasped the point. 'Oh, I am slow indeed! Of course! I know exactly what you mean. Yes!'

'I'm glad you know what he's talking about, Halloran,' the Master said, sounding peevish. 'I can only echo the mayor's question. Why bring up the secret sale of some books?'

'That was how he made sure Bonneviot would go to the right spot at the time when McSwiggan, the assassin, would be waiting. It was but the work of a moment for him to kill Daniel Bonneviot. His son may even have watched him do it. He must have been nearby to pick up the books his father had brought and spirit them away.'

'All this cannot be true!' the mayor protested. 'Hinman and George Bonneviot cannot be the same person.'

'It is true, sir. I had our coroner send for Mrs. Swan and show her the body Brock here identified as Mr. Hinman. She confirmed that it was her step-brother, George Bonneviot.' Once again, for a few moments, all in the room were silent, finally taking in the full cunning and ruthlessness that had been used.

'How could George Bonneviot have fooled us, Foxe?' It was the mayor again, still unwilling to believe what the others could now see plain before them. 'He was born in this city. Grew up here. Many would have known him.'

'The one they knew, Mr. Mayor, was a boy of twelve years old or under. Now he was a man of twenty-four or twenty-five. He had hardly been in this city in the time between. Add his acting skills, fine clothes and perhaps some other tricks of the stage, and he could pass unknown. Especially as no one expected to encounter him. So long as he avoided the few who would know him anywhere, like his step-sister and mother, he could pass amongst us unrecognised. He also took the greatest possible care to establish his new identity beyond doubt. He frequented the coffee houses and meeting places of the city – always amongst relative strangers. There he proclaimed himself to be Mr. James Hinman of Halifax. He could talk wisely about cloth and the cloth-trade, for he had been a journeyman weaver, as well as the son of one of the most prosperous merchants in the city. Nor need he fear mistakes in his knowledge of the north of England and Yorkshire, since that was where he was living. All he had to do was shift the focus to a known centre of worsted manufacture, like Halifax. The rest was easy.'

'Aye,' Brock said. 'I wager he still knew enough of Norwich to be able to find the men he needed. That's how he found Underhill, the forger, and McSwiggan to carry out the murder.'

'And Beeston for the money, Brock. The hundred pounds his father had given him would not go far. He had new clothes to buy and a prosperous lifestyle to maintain. He had to pay men like Underhill and McSwiggan. Beeston was his first bad mistake. I fear it also proved his last.'

'So what was his plan?' Alderman Halloran asked.

'It was simple, yet almost perfect,' Foxe said. 'He would obtain a false bill of sale, so that he could claim the cloth had been sold to him. Not just sold, but – and this was important – sold before his father had contracted any loans. That was why he was so particular in the date he asked Underhill to put upon it. In that way, he could, as Hinman, say that the cloth was already his. Then it would not be included in Bonneviot's estate or fall prey to his creditors. All this he did as Hinman. As George, he could say he had returned to the North after his father disinherited him. That was what we assumed anyway. He was several hundred miles away when the killing and fraud took place. Besides, as you have pointed out, Mr. Mayor, on the face of things his father's death would not benefit him at all. He no longer had an inheritance.'

'What a devil!' the mayor cried. 'To murder his own father for gain!'

'No, sir. Not for gain. For revenge. Revenge for the blows and indignities he must have seen his mother and step-sister endure for many years. Revenge for being sent to London and forced to spend seven years learning a trade he did not like or wish to follow. Revenge above all for his father's disdain and cruel rejection and for his dashed hopes. He had returned in triumph to prove, like father and grandfather, he had made good through his own, unaided effort. Yet his father had treated him with contempt. Daniel Bonneviot caused his own death, you might well say. His many sins caught up with him at last.'

'And you worked out what George was up to and thus allowed us to frustrate it, Foxe,' Alderman Halloran said. 'He must have been going to sell that cloth for whatever he could get, just as the London banker would have done. That would have ruined our trade.'

'I was too slow, I fear, Alderman. I had my suspicions when the business arose of there being no inventory with the bill of sale. Who might know the cloth was in the warehouse, yet be unable to access it to list what was there? I even considered George Bonneviot at the start of this affair, but for the wrong reason. Like everyone else, I accepted the false image of his character. I was told of his determination to become an actor. I knew of the talent the London managers saw in him. Yet I still failed to do more than see both as further proof that he must be away in the North, busy learning his new craft. Had I been quicker to see what was going on, I might have saved George from Beeston's men.'

'You would have only saved him for the hangman, Foxe,' the mayor said.

'True, sir. Yet that would be a quicker and less agonising way to die.'

'Be that as it may, you have our most profound thanks. You have been the means of saving us all from substantial loss. You have also allowed this disgraceful business to remain secret. I charge all of you here present never to speak of what you have heard today. Let the world believe Bonneviot died at the hands of a footpad. His business and estate are already being wound up in the normal way of things. I doubt there will be much money left when all is done, but we will not leave Mrs. Bonneviot without the means of support. That much her son has achieved for her, even if he failed in all the rest.'

'I have also taken the liberty of writing this morning to Mrs. Swan, sir,' Foxe said, 'asking her to tell her step-mother only that some ruffians unknown had killed George. That much is true, after all. I suggested he had returned secretly to Norwich, fearful of his father's wrath. He may even have intended to visit his family again. Unhappily, he had fallen foul of thieves, being but a penniless actor and unable to lodge anywhere but in the worst parts of the city. Such a tale will cause no fuss, only sadness.'

'You have done the right thing, Foxe,' Alderman Halloran said. 'There is no need to cause more distress to Mrs. Bonneviot, nor blacken the name of a family once well-respected in the city. Every large town in the land possesses areas where the criminal classes lurk. Until we can cleanse our realm of such noisome persons, they will commit every foul deed imaginable. Only the most rigorous application of the law can contain them.'

'Speaking of which,' the mayor said, 'I have committed Underhill and McSwiggan for trial at the next assize. I dare say they will trouble us no more. As for Beeston, he is far too cunning a rogue to be taken easily. Yet Providence may yet produce his downfall, as it did for both Bonneviots, father and son.'

The mayor and the Guild Master now took their leave. Foxe and Brock also departed. The Alderman was triumphant. His protégè, Foxe, had delivered everything he had hoped. The mayor was once more indebted to him. And best of all, Mr. Foxe had assured him that he would soon call with several most interesting additions for his library.

Chapter Twenty-Three

The Mayor's Ball

GEORGE BONNEVIOT WAS LAID TO REST IN THE FAMILY PLOT, as far away from his father as might be managed with decency. His step-sister saw to that. She also took care that, in death, he should be treated with all the dignity due to him as a member of the Bonneviot family. Many of the family even made the journey from London once again, mourning son as well as father. Daniel Bonneviot's death had wiped away any lurking doubts about his standing as a merchant and master weaver. Now George was honoured as a successful young actor, denied the career he had craved. Theatrical folk stood alongside sober merchants at the funeral.

Foxe did not attend, nor did Brock. No one must know that they had any part in the events surrounding either death. Instead, they went to Foxe's favourite coffee house and raised a dish of chocolate each to George's memory.

'I believe, in all honesty, that he might have become one of the titans of the stage, Brock, whether as actor or playwright. His one and only performance in this city was masterly on both counts. As Hinman, he convinced us all of his false identity. As the designer of the means of carrying out his plan, while maintaining the fiction that he was far away at the time, he nearly brought off another triumph. Indeed, while I wish the death of no man, I am almost sorry for my part in unmasking his intentions. Daniel Bonneviot, as I told our own audience that day in Alderman Halloran's library, was in large part the cause of his own death. Had it not been for his domineering, tyrannical violence in his home, his wives and children might have loved him. In business too, he gave few any cause to regret his passing. A most quarrelsome and disputatious man! Someone must have struck him down eventually.'

'Did you sell the alderman any books?'

'Oh yes. I never buy a book without knowing at the same time whom I can sell it to, Brock. To have unsold stock on your shelves looks well, but makes no profit. Our good alderman's purse is quite a little lighter, but he is happier for the loss.'

'And yours is even fatter! Though I dare say the Catt sisters will help ease the burden of all those guineas soon enough. It is the Mayor's Ball next week. Which one are you taking?'

'Why, both.'

Foxe's reply caused poor Brock to choke on a mouthful of chocolate, so that it was some moments before he could speak again.

'By God, Foxe! That will cause such a tittle-tattling in the city as will last a full twelve months. Are you serious? To go to the Mayor's Ball in the company of an actress is scarcely pardonable in the eyes of many. To take the madam of a bordello, even if it is both fashionable and patronised by all the quality in the city, will be seen as proof that your soul is damned for all eternity. To take both ... I cannot find the words to describe the uproar it will cause. Does the mayor know what you intend?'

'I think it might best come as a surprise. He might try to stop me otherwise and that I will not allow. I am sure he will cope admirably on the night, even if it will put a sore strain on his heart when he sees us for the first time. He is well used to putting a diplomatic face on situations of extreme embarrassment.'

'Why do you do things like this?'

'Why not? I care not a fig for the niceties of society. Nor for the strictures of the self-righteous. Besides, none can do anything to me, for I have more than enough money to render me immune from their petty displeasure. No, Brock. I will take both ladies because both deserve it. They are beautiful, elegant and well-born. As you well know, their father was amongst the most prosperous local merchants, as is their brother. Even more than that, they are clever and successful in their chosen paths. And most of all, I love them both dearly. What better reasons could you wish for?'

'None, I suppose. I only regret I will not be there to see the expressions of horror on the faces of many present.'

'But you will, Brock. I have purchased a ticket for you too.' Brock could only gape at that. 'I cannot be with both ladies every moment and I would not leave either in the situation of not having a suitable gentleman to escort them. Just about every man in the whole room, be he but wealthy enough, will have enjoyed the services of Gracie's girls on many occasions. Even so, none will dare acknowledge her openly in the presence of their wives and female relatives. They will smile and nod and hope no one notices. Nor will many be willing to be seen with an actress, especially one who is young, beautiful and well-known for taking on many comic and bawdy roles. No, I will rely on you to attend whichever sister I am unable to be with at that point. You do not care about society's strictures any more than I do, Brock. And if any assail you with reproaches, you have my permission to deal with them in whatever way you think fit.'

❧

The evening of the Mayor's Ball proved fine and not too warm. This was counted a great blessing by all who planned to attend. All would be wearing their best clothes. Thus none relished arriving outside the Assembly Rooms in rain and having to hasten inside as best they could. Dancing shoes were not made for damp ground or moving at too fast a pace. Even a shower might mark silks and satins. And as for the magnificent hats and hairstyles …! Most could recall past occasions when the short walk to the entrance had ruined hours of work and a good many guineas' worth of laces and feathers.

Too warm an evening could be almost as bad. So many people and candles in one room always made it uncomfortably hot, whatever the temperature outside. But if the air was warm already, even sitting and talking would cause great discomfort, let alone dancing.

Mindful of the preservation of his guests' outfits, Mr. Foxe had hired a roomy, closed carriage. Now, as this equipage drew up, he swiftly jumped down, ready to hand his ladies down from the carriage and escort them within. As always, a throng of townspeople and loungers were also on hand. All were eager to view the fashions. Many were also ready enough to shout out ribald comments in voices rich with Norfolk dialect.

Foxe's appearance drew a good few appreciative whistles and catcalls. 'Gawd save us!' came one voice from the crowd. 'Is that a man or what? I ain't never seen so many patterns on one suit afore.'

'It's Monsewer Maccaroni, I declare!' another cried in response. 'That do strut round Piccadilly like a cockerel on a dunghill.'

'Naw!' came another voice. 'That's some parrot a sailor 'as brought back from the Indies.'

Predictably, the mob were delighted with the comparison of Foxe's highly decorated clothes to parrot feathers. Now they exploded into cries of 'Pretty Polly!' and 'Oo's a pretty bird, then?'

What silenced them was the appearance of Kitty from the coach. Many knew her from the stage and she was a great favourite. But that night ...! From her tumbling auburn tresses to the dainty shoes in fine brocade that peeped from beneath her petticoat, she was a sight none could see and not fall silent. Her dressmaker had excelled herself in the use of the cloth Foxe had bought. Kitty's dress, styled á la francaise, first clung to her body, then swung out from the waist to reveal a petticoat richly quilted and decorated with tiny bows and trinkets. Diamonds and emeralds glinted in her hair. About her pale and flawless neck hung a slim necklace of emeralds and gold. And from its lowest point, a single, egg-shaped emerald dropped down just far enough to nestle between the tops of her breasts. She was magnificent and she knew it.

Now came her sister, Gracie. She too wore no hat, preferring to allow her rich, dark curls to be dressed into a towering mass, from which peeped pearls and tiny silver bows. Gracie's dress was styled á la polonaise, with flounces and swags on the back and skirt. Around her throat was a choker of pearls with a diamond clasp, while groups of pearls were set over her petticoat and the bodice of her dress. Even her shoes revealed pearl-encrusted buckles. Her neck and shoulders gleamed as lustrous as her pearls, before each eye moved down to glimpse breasts fit to tempt a bishop into sin ... which indeed they had, and more than once.

'Gawd!' came a shout from the crowd. 'It's that bootiful Queen 'o Sheba what tempted Solomon!' Nor was that comparison too far from the mark. There was something so rich and exotic about Gracie Catt that not a few seemed ready to bow or curtsy as she swept past them.

Foxe had been steeling himself all day for the response he was likely to meet when he entered the hall with these two ladies beside him. For himself, he was supremely indifferent to the disapproval of the self-righteous. Yet he was determined his guests should not have their evening spoiled by the vicious remarks he knew some people in the city were capable of throwing out. He thought he could trust the mayor to maintain a politician's calm appearance under pressure. Besides, the man owed him a great deal and would be unlikely to forget it. Alderman Halloran was another who could be relied upon. For the rest ... well, he would see.

He need not have worried, since fate was about to throw him such a gift as he could never have imagined. As his party neared the door – Brock bringing up the rear in glum silence – a familiar voice called out.

'I say, Foxe. Nearly didn't recognise you in all that finery. And who are these two veritable angels alongside you?'

The Eighth Earl of Pentelow, accompanied by three other people, stood before them. From the look on his face, he had no idea who Foxe's companions were and probably cared less. All he saw were two women of extraordinary beauty. Nothing else would matter.

'My Lord.' Foxe bowed elegantly. 'May I present Miss Catt and her sister Miss Catherine Catt, and my good friend Captain Brock? Ladies, this is His Lordship, the Eighth Earl of Pentelow.'

'You certainly may, Foxe. Damn me, ladies, you're enough to take my breath away. Whatever are you doing with a dull stick like Foxe here? Come and join us. You too ... er ... Brock, of course.'

Kitty and Gracie curtsied most gracefully, neither at all put out by His Lordship's evident wish to look as closely at the necklines of their dresses as he could without falling over. Indeed, he was so intent on leering over the Catt sisters that Foxe had to rescue him from the grave impropriety of failing to introduce his own companions.

'And your guests, My Lord?'

'Ah … what? Oh, yes. May I present my sister-in-law, Lady Henfield. M'wife's indisposed, y'know.' From the look Lady Henfield – a tall, plain young woman with large eyes but no chest worth speaking of – gave the earl, there was little affection between them. 'This is my cousin, Henry, Marquis of Chermouth, and his wife, Emma. Now, ladies. Let's go inside and find you some refreshment.' Then, in an aside to Foxe clearly designed for them all to hear, His Lordship added, 'Never thought you had it in you, Foxe. Couple of amazing beauties like these. Quite made my evening.'

Thus, now in a group of eight containing two peers of the realm, Foxe, Brock and the Catt sisters were swept inside. Gasps there were – though they could be taken as expressions of admiration – and shaken heads. Yet none would dare to offer the Earl of Pentelow and his party any insult. Least of all the mayor, who hurried over, bowing and simpering in the manner of any politician confronted by someone of far superior status. Nor Alderman Halloran. His whole mouth hung open for nearly a minute, before he recollected himself and hastened over as well. Both intended to bask in the celebrity of this party who were so much the centre of attention that even the orchestra lost the time of their music for a few bars.

'I must say,' Brock commented to Foxe later, 'in your case the devil not only looks after 'is own, he makes sure 'e 'as the best of everything.'

'Enjoying yourself, Brock?' Foxe said.

'I am indeed. Didn't think I would, mind. I likes Gracie well enough and she seems to like me, even though I'm far beneath her usual standard of companion. Kitty is a sweet little minx who no one could dislike. But that Lady Henfield … She's quite a woman, believe me. May not look much, but she's got a brain that's as good as any two men. She's 'ad me laughing most of the evening. Wit? You've never 'eard the like! Of course, she loathes her brother-in-law and says 'e treats his wife badly. Always off gambling and chasing women. Still, that's the aristocracy for you.'

'I noticed she seemed to be spending a good deal of time in your company, Brock.'

'Well … you were looking after your Catt women well enough, I thought. When you could prise the earl and his cousin off 'em. I did ask Julia …um, Lady Henfield … whether we should make sure to spend time with Marchioness Chermouth. But she said the silly woman likes nothing better than to be a martyr to her husband's wandering eye. It's her only topic of conversation, seemingly.'

'So what did you and Her Ladyship talk about, Brock?'

'Ships and the sea, mostly. She asked me a heap of questions and seemed to have a real interest.'

Foxe's loud laughter affronted Brock.

'What's wrong wi' that? I said she's a bright one. Why shouldn't she want to know about navigation and foreign parts and the like?'

'No reason at all, Brock. Forgive me. Now, I suggest you hurry back to Her Ladyship … Julia, I believe you said. The evening is far from over and I doubt the earl will spare her a single thought. Here, take these glasses of champagne. Have you asked her to dance with you yet?'

'Twice, if you must know. And she did. Said I moved most gracefully for a big man.'

Now it was Foxe's turn to berate himself inside his head. He fell too easily into seeing Brock as the blunt, simple man he pretended to be. To make it worse, he knew it was not true. Brock was probably at least as wealthy as many an alderman and far more successful in business matters.

'So you do, Brock. I'm glad you're enjoying yourself. I count it the best proof of Lady Julia Henfield's intelligence and perception that she has seen through your defences to what is beneath. Go to her! Go! Here comes the earl again and I must hasten to whisk one of the sisters onto the dance floor and away from his wandering hands. Ah, there is Kitty, safely talking to the mayor and his wife. I wager she will inveigle the mayor into dancing the moment she sees the earl approaching. Now where is Gracie?'

Foxe never knew if the Earl of Pentelow discovered he had spent the evening ogling an actress and the madam of a fashionable bordello. Nor if he cared. It was enough that the Catt sisters had enjoyed a fine evening of company. They had drawn more admiring looks and comments than any of the other women present, and done so without encountering snubs or rudenesses. Much would be said behind their backs, of course, but, all in all, he could feel well satisfied. And as for Brock and Lady Henfield …

No, it had been a great success. And if that was due to the devil, as Brock suggested, Foxe would happily continue to be one of his own and enjoy it.

Made in the USA
San Bernardino, CA
08 September 2018